MW00416309

Highland Essence
Book Two
Highland Treasures

highland essence

highland treasures

book two

by

c.a. szarek

Paper Dragon Publishing

Highland Essence
C.A. Szarek

Highland Treasures Book Two

All rights reserved
Copyright © October, 2022, C.A. Szarek
Cover Photograph Copyright © August, 2017 Period Images, V.J. Dunraven
Cover Model: Julie Paige
Cover Design Copyright © 2017, Bookin' It Designs, Talina Perkins
Series Logo Design Copyright © 2016, Danielle Loiselle
Edited by Susan Sheehey

Paper Dragon Publishing
North Richland Hills, TX

Names, characters and incidents depicted in this book are products of the author's imagination, or are used fictitiously. Any resemblance to actual events, locales, organizations, or persons, living or dead, is entirely coincidental and beyond the intent of the author or the publisher.

No part of this book may be reproduced or shared by any electronic or mechanical means, including, but not limited to printing, file sharing, and email, without prior written permission from Paper Dragon Publishing or the Author.

eBook ISBN: 978-1-941151-41-9
Print book ISBN: 978-1-941151-42-6

First eBook Edition: October, 2022
First Print Edition: October, 2022

other books by c.a. szarek

<u>Highland Secrets Trilogy</u> — Fantasy/Paranormal
<u>Romance</u>

The Princess and The Laird (Highland Secrets Prequel)
The Fae Ring (Book Two)
The Parchment Scroll (Book Three)
Highland Valentine (A Highland Secrets HEA Story)
Highlander's Portrait (A Highland Secrets Story)

<u>Highland Treasures</u> — Fantasy/Paranormal Romance

Highland Oath (Book One)
Highland Essence (Book Two)

<u>The King's Riders</u> — Fantasy Romance

Sword's Call (Book One)
Love's Call (Book Two)
Rogue's Call (Book Three)
Fate's Call (A Novella from the World of the King's
Riders)

<u>Crossing Forces</u> — Romantic Suspense

Collision Force (Book One)
Cole in Her Stocking (A Crossing Forces Christmas) —
FREE read!
Chance Collision (Book Two)

Calculated Collision (Book Three)
Collision Control (Book Four)
Weekend Collision (A Crossing Forces HEA Story) —
FREE read!
Superior Collision (Book Five)
Incendiary Collision (Book Six) — *Coming Soon!*

The Giovanni

King of Hearts (Book One)
Queen of Diamonds (Book Two) — *Coming Soon!*

Dedication

I started writing this book about three years ago, and then life happened. During the ups and downs, there were points I was convinced I would never finish another book, let alone publish one.

So, I supposed this book is dedicated to perseverance. No matter what happens, if you fight for what you want hard enough, it can be a reality.

Here's to this book, story and *this* "the end."
I will do I again, too! I hope you love Lexi and Graeme as much as I do!

chapter one

*a*ct like a grown woman.

Her mother's voice resounded in her head. Their telepathic communication was one of things she needed to escape. Lexi ignored her mother's urgings in her mind.

Get out of my head, she shouted back.

Fury guided her actions more than the magic flowing over her in waves. She cursed under her breath, using words she'd never had the courage to voice. Things a proper lady would never deign to say. Even at one and twenty, her father would take her to task. Threaten to tan her hide like he would a lad.

She had no care; only continued the rhythmic actions of her flying fingers, the first requirements to open the Faery Stones. She sensed the music greeting her, yet she couldn't smile. Magic usually calmed her, but the rage at her mother — her entire family, really — drove her.

Lexi needed to get away.

Away from their chiding. Away from their smothering. From the constant overprotection, as if she was a lassie instead of a grown woman.

Alana, her mother went on, in full lecture mode, but she whispered a spellword to eject her from her mind.

She wasn't acting like an adult.

She was proving her mother right. Letting impulsivity and anger guide her, but she didn't stop what she was doing.

Lexi *couldn't*.

As the daughter of a former Fae princess, she was half Fae, and she *deserved* her legacy. The magic in front of her, in the form of the Faery Stones was a part of her heritage.

She was a much a part of the Fae world as the human one.

Or she *should* be. Lexi had a *right* to what was before her.

The Faery Stones were made up of five clustered natural formations, rising from the small cavern's floor, perfectly spaced from each other in a loose circle. One was centered with the other four surrounding it.

When she'd rushed into the dark cave, her eyes hadn't required time to adjust, because the magic before her lit up the caverns, chasing away the shadows.

The crystals glinted, as if some light source was present to reflect off them, but the radiance came from *inside* the gems. The Stones gave off enough light to illuminate the cave, but they were hidden well enough to prevent unexpected guests.

No one would find this location along the beaches of Skye, unless they knew where to look.

Her mother had charms in place to deter humans from stumbling upon it. Even if they had no magic, there was an overwhelming sense of dread that settled over any person in the vicinity.

Lexi felt it too, but the call of the Stones to her Fae side always overrode it. Like her mother, she had a strong tie to the crystals.

She could feel the melody. She'd always heard the song they played; the internal tune danced in her thoughts, drawing her closer, as if by instinct, and steered her movements as she repeated the pattern — touching each crystal — that would open the portal.

Each Stone sat atop the five naturally formed pillars, and were from the Realm of the Fae; magic-born. The largest one in the center was the key to making the others work. They had to be in sync as a whole to open the portal.

The semi-circle the Faery Stones sat in was perfect, as if it had been placed there, not grown. That was probably the case; they'd been put in the Human Realm a millennia ago by Fae who'd wanted to link their worlds, for unknown reasons; perhaps to explore?

Learning how to open them didn't come naturally to those with Fae lineage, as it did to Lexi. Usually, it took several tries to get it right; but not her. She'd always felt their melody in her blood and had been able to open them the first time she'd tried — much to her mother's chagrin.

The main Stone called to her, brightening and thrumming. Power coursed through her, making her limbs buzz. The pleasure of it fought the negative feelings still filtering through her system.

She bounced on her heels, and her feet slid around in the too-big deerskin boots. They were certainly improper footwear for *her*, but she hadn't taken time to use the shrinking spellword her cousin had taught her. The boots also belonged to him, but hopefully Liam wouldn't be to upset she'd stolen them.

That tiny bit of magic was handy, given that she had a penchant for *borrowing* lad's clothes whenever she fled home. Something her mother accused her of doing far too often.

The trews she wore fit like they belonged to her, but they too, were stolen. The deep purple hue was made of fine material from the Fae Realm. Her mother was fond of them, and would be even more irritated when she realized they were missing.

Lexi hummed to the notes each crystal emitted. The Stones responded by going radiant, and the trill got louder, making her body vibrate.

Warmth shot through her, traveling up her fingers, into her wrists and limbs. A welcome feeling dimming more of her anger.

The first *pop* sounded, indicating the portal's advent. Then the familiar sound of tearing parchment.

The following *pop-pop-pop* was each louder than the last, and a magic-born gale swirled around her, making her hair fly in her face.

The flow of power worked up more heat inside her, and the moving air was like a caress, offering blissful coolness even if her tresses stung her eyes.

White light shot straight up to the cave's ceiling from the center crystal of the Faery Stones, the last occurrence before the portal's birth.

The same had happened when she and Liam had opened the Stones almost two years before.

Anticipation hit her, and she broke physical contact with the final crystal.

Alexandria.

Her given name held warning and alarm. Her mother was attuned to the magic of the Faery Stones, even more so than she or her brother, so it wasn't a surprise that Alana would know what she was doing.

It also wasn't a surprise her mother had obliterated her mental block. The former princess was a powerful empath.

Alexandria Evelyn Claire MacLeod.

Lexi shook her head as her mother's assumed omnipotence hitched up a few notches with her entire Christian name. It contained more than alarm.

There was real fear there.

Tales she'd been told of the ferocious Fae danced through her head.

That should give her pause—

An iridescent orb appeared, distracting her from her own bud of doubt and distress. The whole cavern shimmered and wavered as the glowing bubble grew.

The opening hovered above the stark white sand littering the floor of the cave, and the light reflected off it.

Then the portal floated downward, hovering a few inches in the air.

At first hazy and opaque, it started to clear, like multicolored clouds retreating. It grew larger and larger by the second.

Soon, it would reveal the realm on the other side.

The Fae Realm.

The doorway would take her to the people of her mother, and she cared not that it was supposedly dangerous.

Her cousin Liam—the son of a former Fae Warrior—had told her of his adventures when he'd snuck into the other side.

Multiple times.

Like his father Xander, her cousin had wings in the realm of the Fae, unlike here, on the Isle of Skye, in the human world.

As her blasted mother had always explained it, the world of the humans had much less magic, so her cousins—father and son alike—didn't have their wings.

Over there, Liam could *fly*.

Over there, her powers would come more easily.

Lexi had been cautioned her whole life how dangerous the Fae were. How they could sense human blood and would kill her on sight for being an abomination, for intruding in their world. Her father Alex, the current Laird MacLeod, was human.

Her mother had sadly explained that her grandfather, the King of the Scottish Fae, Fillan, wouldn't suffer to look at her before he had her killed, regardless of their blood tie.

Alana had forever fled her people to be with Lexi's father, so the same was true for the former princess. She was exiled. Self-banished, since she'd fled imprisonment before Lexi's birth.

Banishment was preferred to being killed by one's own blood, her mother always said. She was also fond of adding, had they not escaped together—since the king had also taken Alex hostage—Lexi would likely have never been born.

Neither Lexi, nor her brother, Angus, had ever been to the Realm of the Fae.

Liam had always managed to get away from the Fae Warriors who supposedly guarded the Faery Stones on the other side. He knew spells they'd played with as wee ones; knew how to turn invisible for a short time.

They both knew some defensive magic forbidden to use at home. Her mother frowned upon most, if not all, magic use.

Lexi wouldn't focus on that now, or what'd happened to cause her flight from Dunvegan.

She could *blink*, or travel by picturing her destination, and appearing there by will. Her Aunt Claire called it traveling telepathically.

She'd get away, too.

Lexi.

This time, the voice in her head was her brother's.

She swallowed.

With the nickname Aunt Claire had given her, she could feel Angus' censure, but also his compassion and worry. His love for her.

So, *he* was going to be the one to try to reason with her. A good plan, since she tended to hear her brother out before she would their parents.

Not today.

She spat a word she'd learned from her Aunt Jules, and had been told by Claire *never* to utter.

It seemed as if all her ladylike sensibilities had fled.

Lexi grinned for the first time since she'd run out of

the bailey and down the road, headed to the beach. She'd fled on foot, since she'd been worried her beloved mount, her silver mare, Turadh, would've been lost had she taken time to get her from the stables.

The waiting portal glimmered, as if beckoning her.

She couldn't make out what was on the other side; it was too dark.

No matter.

With a quick prayer and a big calming breath, she stepped into the bubble.

"Stubborn old fool." Graeme stomped his foot, then froze. He was thirty years old, dammit. He shouldn't be stalking the beach like a child, kicking rocks. He hadn't pouted since he was small, or, *wee,* as the locals would say.

Despite the relatively warm morning, the overcast sky threatened a thunderstorm.

He stared out at the water. The waves crashed into the shore with an edge of violence, each larger than the last, seeming as angry as he was.

Well, *angry* was too strong a word.

He was frustrated with his grandfather. The man wouldn't listen, no matter what. It was as if he held a grudge against Graeme that *he* could never be at fault for.

It was no secret James MacDonald had never wanted his son, Craig, Graeme's father, to marry his American bride, Susan, and move to Texas.

Away from Scotland. Away from their ancestral

home on the Isle of Skye.

It wasn't *his* fault.

He hadn't even been born.

Graeme had only met the Scottish guy a few times when he was a kid—he'd spent a few summers in on the Isle of Skye—but now his parents were gone, and he'd just wanted to reconnect with the only family he had left. Immediate family, anyway.

His mother's family, his two aunts, two uncles and a smattering of cousins were alive and thriving at home, most of them in the Dallas area.

His mother had met his father because she'd gone to college in Scotland.

Graeme had toyed with the idea of moving to Scotland after he'd sold his father's lucrative construction company.

A fucking drunk driver had ruined his life three years ago, when the bastard had hit his parents, and although he'd worked for his dad for a few years, his degree was in architecture—a result of his mother's urging—so he hadn't wanted to run the business permanently.

As much as he enjoyed designing buildings, his passion was something his grandfather was coincidentally renowned for. Restoration.

He'd seen pictures of his grandfather's projects and been fascinated. Graeme had worked for a pretty prominent architecture firm after college, and helped his dad on the side, but his penchant for buying antique furniture that needed some TLC had been his in-the-garage thing for years, too.

His mother had teased he was wasting his talent, but she'd loved the pieces he'd given her all the same.

Damn, he missed his parents.

He couldn't close his eyes without seeing their smiling faces, so perhaps a small part of him had needed that from James, as well.

When the hospital had called after Gramps' fall almost six months before, he'd panicked; convinced he'd lose the last of his father's blood, even though he hadn't seen his grandfather since he was a teen.

Too bad his image was shattered by the curmudgeon who'd greeted him in that tiny hospital room after his hip replacement surgery.

James MacDonald was a bitter old man, and evidently Graeme had only made it worse with his appearance. He looked just like his father, and James had declared him an unwanted reminder of the past, a reminder of the son he'd considered lost, when in reality, Gramps had wasted time until it was too late.

"I'm right here, Gramps." The wind whipped away his whisper.

He'd wanted to learn from a master.

His grandfather wasn't just good at restoring furniture, he'd worked on historical sites, castles, and was a well-informed historian. He'd worked with teams as little as two, and as large as directing hundreds of men, not just in Scotland, but all over the UK.

The man was a legend. The master of his rare craft.

He was the one they called when old things needed to look new again but needed to maintain their authenticity.

Too bad James MacDonald knew every damn thing, and didn't want to be told a damn thing.

Graeme had wanted to help him be more efficient, upgrade his business, new accounting software, maybe a CRM, money saving tips, but Gramps wouldn't listen.

If he had to hear, "I've been runnin' this business fer fifty years. What would a lad like ye know?" one more time, he might scream.

Like a girl.

The man was insufferable.

Just as stubborn as his son.

Graeme and his dad had had a healthy row from time to time, so it looked like *stubborn* was just in the blood, confirming his mother's constant declaration.

Damn, if Mom could see us now.

Graeme smiled, even if it probably carried the sadness he felt for his loss. His grandfather felt it, too, even if he never talked about it.

The older man could barely look at pictures of the man, even though they were everywhere in his house. He would frown, and obviously avoid glancing at framed images, as if Craig's smile would morph to a look of disapproval.

His grandfather had lost his son way before Graeme had lost his dad. Even if it'd been the codger's choice.

Another sigh floated from his mouth and he shook his head.

He might as well crawl back to Dunvegan Castle and muster some semblance of an apology. God knew his grandfather never would, even if harsh words were flung on both sides.

They were working on a small restoration project in the seven-hundred-year-old castle that belonged to Clan MacLeod. It wasn't the older man's first go at the castle. He'd been a key part of the ten-year long major restoration all over the MacLeod stronghold that had finished a few years before.

Well, *Gramps* was working. He wouldn't let Graeme do much more than watch, despite his training and experience in construction and architecture, or his dabbling in restoration. The stubborn jerk barely let him bring in supplies from the truck, even the heavy stuff.

Bridget, the young woman who worked for his grandfather part-time in the office, always said he'd die on the job because he never asked for help.

Graeme disagreed.

James MacDonald was too obstinate to die.

With a few curses for good measure, he kicked at the loamy ground and watched the dirt, sand and pebbles fly forward. The wind assisted, carrying off the lighter particles until he couldn't see them anymore.

The scent of the sea tickled his nose.

He kicked again, this time harder, throwing up more small rocks and sending them off to new homes.

"Ow."

He stilled. A random voice on a deserted beach?

His ears had to be deceiving him.

Graeme scanned the area in front of him. There was a small ridge he couldn't see around unless he descended a yard or so.

Was that a foot?

He scrambled down, making more dirt and rocks

shift beneath him.

There was definitely movement there, and that foot was bare, as was the shapely calf attached to it.

He kept going until she was in view, then skidded to a halt.

Not only were her feet and legs bare...so was the rest of her.

Completely.

Naked.

No doubt, the form was female. A *stunning* female.

Graeme chided himself for checking out the curve of her ass, but since she was lying on her side, he didn't have much of a choice.

Until she rolled to her back and put her hand to her forehead, revealing almost everything else.

Her breasts were small and high, and she had long dark hair. She had one leg bent, and one straight, obscuring his view of her, well, most private place, but he could barely tear his eyes away.

Because despite the fact that something had obviously happened to her, what he could see was pretty perfect.

He kicked his ass into gear and clambered to her side. "Are you all right?"

When she didn't immediately move, he squatted down.

"Miss?"

She moved her arm away from her face and blinked up at him. "What?" The question was whispered, but revealed a brogue.

Funny, he could hear it from one word, and it'd

become so…normal.

He'd been in Scotland for almost eight months now, and loved everything about the country, its people, the wonderful accent.

Even his stubborn grandfather.

"Are you okay?" Graeme repeated.

Her gaze seemed to zone in on him for the first time. Big. Violet. Eyes.

Like practically purple.

How weird.

Contacts?

He cleared his throat. "Miss?"

She coughed and tried to sit up, but struggled, as if she couldn't get the job done.

"I'm gonna grab your arm, okay, ma'am? Help you up?"

Her skin was soft beneath his fingertips and a shiver ran up his shoulder and down his spine, almost snapping him to attention.

She must've felt it, too, because those unusual eyes collided with his again. She licked her lips, and he had the odd desire to lean down and taste her mouth.

Graeme shook himself and studied her face.

She was exquisite, and it wasn't just those eyes, or the rest of her body. Her high cheekbones and full lips accentuated her heart-shaped face.

This female was the whole package.

He helped her to shaking legs, and grabbed her elbows to steady her. He couldn't tear his eyes from her slender waist or the curve of her delectably rounded hips.

Graeme forbade himself from looking further south.

Her locks were so dark, ebony, skimming her hips in the gentle breeze.

Her nipples were pebbled, and oh-so perfect. Her breasts would fit wholly in his hands, and that'd always been his favorite kind of woman.

Oh geeze, stop being a perv.

She was cold, from her overly pale and goosebump-covered skin. Graeme needed to help her. Definitely needed to stop looking at her tits, before his dick got ideas. A boner in tight jeans was no friend of his.

He'd already had the desire to press his lips to hers, and he'd never kissed a stranger in his life. He didn't need any *other* ideas.

"What happened to you?" Graeme asked. "Did someone hurt you?" He scanned her alabaster skin—for bruises, he insisted to his inner pervert—but there didn't seem to be a mark on her.

"Yer no' Scottish," she blurted.

Her brogue was as thick as he'd suspected, and somehow added to her appeal.

Of course, being gorgeous and naked didn't hurt a damn thing.

Graeme smiled. "I am, actually. But I was born and raised in Texas." He whipped his shirt off and handed it to her.

The girl stood staring at his offering; her cheeks pink. "Yer attire is…odd." She looked him up and down, then glanced at his gray tee.

He didn't miss her gaze spending a few seconds too long on his bare torso. The idea that she might like what she saw kicked up his fascination with her.

"*Your* clothes are absent, so you should put this on."

Those eyes landed on his face again, and went so wide he could see her whites. "My...my clothes." That pale flawless skin played ghost and she swayed on her feet.

"Whoa. Just breathe." Graeme grabbed her wrist and drew her into his chest. His shirt fell to the sandy ground.

She gasped as her naked flesh hit his, and he had to bite back a groan when those perfect breasts pressed into him.

Her ending up in his arms hadn't been the plan. He'd just wanted to prevent her from falling over, but damn, he wasn't going to complain.

She was fitted to him and her arms tentatively encircled his waist. She was petite; the top of her head only skimmed the underside of his chin, but he could pull her closer, tuck her into him and she could put her cheek on his pec.

Graeme wanted to hold her. Tighter. As if it was somehow right, and he had the strange notion, he didn't want to let her go.

"Warm," she whispered.

Her breathy exclamation somehow kicked in his manners.

"Oh. Shit, I'm sorry. Let's get my shirt on you." He kept one hand on her forearm so she wouldn't keel over, but really, it was because he couldn't seem to stop touching her now that he'd started.

He swallowed. Twice.

There was definite interest from Mr. Happy, and the dude needed to calm down.

Sure, he hadn't gotten laid in a while, but a reaction like this to a strange woman just because she was naked was a bit uncalled for.

Especially given she was in some kind of trouble. People didn't just show up naked on the beach, after all.

She stared into his face as Graeme lifted her arm like a toddler and slid his short-sleeved T-shirt up to her slender shoulder. She still hadn't looked away when the soft material was over her head, and he gently lifted her hair and let the length tumble down her back. The oversized material stopped mid-thigh on her, and he was ashamed of himself that he wished it was higher — or gone.

"What happened to you?" Graeme asked for the second time, needing the distraction.

Be-freaking-have. You're not a teenager.

The young woman looked at him again, but those fathomless eyes didn't stay put.

He followed her gaze when she whirled from him.

She seemed to study the terrain, the rushing waves, and lastly, his grandfather's blue pickup, parked about fifty feet from the beach.

When she faced him again, her pallor was back, with a touch of fear in her expression.

Graeme's protective instincts flared and he wanted to grab her up, hold her away from the world; keep her safe from whatever obviously scared her.

She swallowed, and he wanted to kiss her throat.

"Could ye kindly tell me tha year?"

chapter two

Something had gone very, *very* wrong.

She wasn't in the Fae Realm.

Lexi tried to stave off the panic slithering up her spine. She glanced at the very tall, sandy-haired man who'd given her the odd-looking leine to don.

His light locks made his very dark brown eyes even more startling, and his obvious concern made her want to squirm.

His large warm hand was still locked on her arm, and a part of her wanted to pull away, but the other part wanted to be up against his bare chest again.

Tremors threatened to take over her body. She'd never been skin-to-skin with a man before. Not like *that,* anyway. Her breasts had touched his defined pectoral and abdominal muscles.

Lexi had wanted more. Wanted him to hold her tight, or lower his head and press his mouth to hers.

She swallowed as her emotions warred within her. She wasn't frightened of him, but she suspected when she'd opened the Faery Stones, it'd ripped open a doorway into time. Because this wasn't 1694 anymore.

The concept wasn't something unfamiliar to her or her family. Her sister-by-marriage had come through the Stones in Lexi's and Liam's botched attempt to go to the

Fae Realm almost two years ago.

Lila was from the far future, a century over three hundred years ahead of her own. She was a surgeon who'd fallen in love with Angus, and decided to stay.

She was a skilled healer, and people from all over came to see her for illness or injury. She'd opened what she called *a clinic* at Dunvegan. She'd also saved Lexi's da from a complicated leg break after being thrown from his horse.

Lexi's two aunts, Claire, and her sister Jules had also time traveled, stayed in her century, and married Highlanders.

What had happened to *her*?

Had Lexi traveled through time as well? Only this time, *forward*?

She recalled all the cautions she'd heard over the years about someone of mixed blood using the Stones.

It didn't *always* result in opening the way to the Fae Realm.

Sometimes it ripped open a hole in time.

Lexi looked around, her eyes landing on the large blue...*thing* on the edge of the beach, then back at the shirtless man.

His trews were odd. They weren't made of hide or linen, like the trews the men in her family wore when they weren't in tartan patterns. They were also blue, and he wore boots like she'd never seen, with a thick dark sole, like he'd stepped in tar and molded it to the bottom of his foot.

She'd come to the future.

It was a logical conclusion, as her cousin-by-blood,

uncle-by-marriage, Xander, Liam's father, would say.

The man tilted his head, studying her, although their eyes hadn't met again. She could feel that dark gaze on her naked form and she quivered.

Not because she was cold, because his garment helped.

It was some kind of awareness, and her gut told her he felt it, too.

The first time they'd touched, it'd been like a magical bolt down her arms. Her belly had warmed, as if she'd had a sip of her father's favorite whisky.

Her companion had asked her what'd happened several times, but she didn't know what to tell him, so she hadn't said a word.

Then again, he'd not answered her inquiry about the current year.

When their eyes finally met again, Lexi startled and bit back a gasp.

He was so handsome. His bare trunk was made up of defined lines and bulging muscles. His biceps were much the same, and he had markings on both upper arms...a painted picture of some sort. She didn't want to stare, so she didn't look long enough to make out the designs.

Her Aunt Claire had a similar painting on her ankle, a permanent one. She called it a *tattoo*. Perhaps these were the same.

She forced her eyes off his expanse of flesh, but she wanted to study the sparse sandy hair across his pectorals, and the one dividing his abdominals and disappearing into his pants.

The hair between his nipples had tickled her cheek when he'd held her, and Lexi had wanted to burrow closer.

To a stranger?

Even a kind one?

Although she'd seen many shirtless men, she'd never been...drawn to one. The men of her clan often sparred wearing only their plaids in the courtyards of Dunvegan.

She'd never wanted to touch a man. Rub up against one. Not in an innocent way, like when she'd embraced her father or brother, uncles or male cousins.

Lexi was...attracted...to this tall kind stranger.

She had to swallow again.

Her mother would call her foolish. She'd done a reckless, stupid thing in opening the Faery Stones, and she was *attracted* to the first person she'd run into? Perhaps the travel through time had messed with her head.

Lexi could hear her mother's ridicule.

Perhaps she was still more bairn than woman, after all.

Not that she'd ever tell her mother *that* idea had danced across her mind.

She should dash down the beach, find the Stones and go home. It wouldn't take long for her magic to seek them out.

But...

Why go back to arguments and disdain?

Of course, she'd have to go home eventually, but she didn't want to *now*.

Guilt churned in her gut.

Her family would worry.

Whether she'd ended up in the forbidden Realm of the Fae, or here in the future, her mother would be *'freaking out,'* as Aunt Claire would say.

Lexi should care, and she *did*.

However, she didn't want to go back.

She'd been accused of being selfish many times, so perhaps she could prove she was indeed…if just a touch?

The man was looking at her expectantly.

Why?

They stared at each other, as if waiting for the other to speak first.

"Ye…ye are…American?" she finally stammered.

Like the women who'd time-traveled and joined her family. She'd heard all about what they called, *the Colonies* in her time, and the other place the man had mentioned, Texas. It was where her aunts and sister-by-marriage were from as well.

Aunt Claire had explained there were fifty states in her time, not just Texas, although it was much larger than Scotland.

If it was an odd coincidence that they were all from the same place, like this tall man, Lexi would leave that to mystery.

Her mother was fond of calling it fate.

Was it *her* fate to come here and meet a man from Texas?

"Yes." He nodded, making his mussed golden brown locks shift.

Lexi had to quash the urge to shy away from him. It

highland essence   31

was as if he'd answered her thought, instead of her verbal inquiry, and *that* notion made her belly warm.

On the other hand, the more she watched his soft-looking hair, the more she wanted to run her fingers through it; so much so, her digits tingled.

She cleared her throat. "What is tha year, if ye please."

His fair brows drew tight, as if the question confused him.

It *was* odd, but she couldn't tell him *why* she was asking. He was, after all, a stranger. If she confessed she'd come from the year 1694 through magic called the Faery Stones, he'd likely declare her mad.

Aunt Claire had told her no one in the future believed in magic anymore, let alone the Fae.

"What happened to you?" the man repeated for the fourth or fifth time.

She held his gaze and forced a shrug. "I need ta know tha year."

It seemed their conversation was destined to consist of them repeating themselves while the other declined to answer.

He tilted his head again, like her little cousin Iain was prone to do.

Thinking of that particular cousin made the argument with her mother come rushing back.

Hurt, mixed with the familiar anger toward the woman who'd birthed her, danced into her mind. This time, it wasn't *just* her mother; it'd been her da, as well as Uncle Duncan and Aunt Claire *all* agreeing.

All joining against her.

Lexi hadn't apologized then, nor would she think it now.

She'd had to save Iain.

How would her aunt and uncle have felt if their youngest son had died?

She didn't regret her actions, no matter how her family had fussed.

Yelled.

Commanded.

Her handsome companion spoke, yanking her from the tormented memories.

Just as well.

She could only deal with one crisis at a time.

The year floated from his full mouth, and although he'd confirmed her suspicions, hearing it wasn't easy.

"Pardon?" she managed.

He repeated himself, then asked, "Why?"

The man had stated a date three hundred plus years from when she'd awoken that morning.

Lexi wavered on her bare feet, but the man's large hand shot out and steadied her. Again.

"Thank ye," she whispered, ignoring his inquiry.

"Anytime." He smiled and something about it made her insides wobble.

He hesitated, as if he wanted to add words, but didn't.

No matter, she still couldn't tell him the truth. Her knees wobbled. She told herself it was the shock of time traveling.

"You gonna be okay?" The concern was back in those alluring midnight eyes.

She forced a nod. She'd have to be.

Lexi scanned the beach again, trying to locate familiar terrain. She didn't spot the large boulder that sat outside the entrance of the cave of the Faery Stones, nor the high ridge that marked the place from a distance.

She didn't feel her mother's *stay-out* charms.

How far had she wandered down the beach?

Or had the topography changed over the centuries?

Had the magic burned out?

Panic jumped up from the pit of her stomach, making her heart thunder.

Obviously, the Faery Stones were still around, or she couldn't be where—*when*—she stood, but what if she couldn't find them to get home?

"Hey," the man whispered. "Where'd you go?"

His calm voice compelled her to look at him again.

Lexi had to clear her throat again before she could speak. "I am braw."

"Good. Okay. Are you hurt?"

"Nay."

"That's good, too." He gave another smile and, her heart skipped all over again. He shoved out his hand. "Graeme MacDonald. You are?"

Oh, Jesu, as her brother would say.

The first person she'd run into was a MacDonald.

"Alex...andria Mac...Leod. My family calls me Lexi." The pretty young woman stuttered and turned bright red, yanking out from under his grip on her arm.

Through her brogue and broken words, he'd been able to make out her name.

"Lexi, huh? That's cute." Graeme smiled.

Lexi's throat worked, as if she was suddenly afraid of him.

Why?

Had a man hurt her, despite her denial?

His mind went to filling in all sorts of forbidden blanks, unwanted reasons she was naked on the beach.

The ideas spawned horrible ideas churning low in his stomach. The very possibilities of such depravities...

"Did you say MacLeod?" he forced out, focusing on her surname.

She looked even more nervous, fidgeting. "Aye."

Graeme thumbed toward the truck. "My grandfather and I are doing some restoration work at Dunvegan. Do you live around here? I can take you home."

"Dun...Dunvegan...is still here." It sounded like a question, but was presented as a statement, as if she'd remembered something she'd forgotten. Her unusual eyes were wide again, and her expression seemed to be of wonder and surprise.

Maybe a bit of pride?

That's odd.

As if *anything* about finding her was normal.

"Umm, yeah. The work is minor, on the main floor in the entrance hall."

She nodded, but somehow Graeme could tell she hadn't really comprehended.

If he'd learned anything since he'd been in Scotland,

sometimes things were lost in translation, even if both parties spoke the same language.

"Are you sure you're okay? Do you need to go to the hospital?"

Lexi cocked her head to one side. "Hospital?"

He blinked. "Yeah. Do you need a doctor?" He cringed, his gut kicking up those earlier dreaded worries. He didn't want to ask if she'd been raped. The idea made him want to stab the would-be perpetrator with a vehemence that went beyond Good Samaritan.

"Oh. Nay." She shook her head, making that long dark hair dance.

He wanted to run his fingers through it.

"Uh, I hate to ask, but did someone…hurt…you?"

Her brow furrowed. "Nay. Why?"

"You were…naked on the beach. Laying there as if unconscious."

Had she been with friends? Drinking and passed out?

He discarded the idea. Graeme might not know her, but she didn't seem the type.

"Oh." She swallowed again, working that throat he wanted to plaster his lips to. "Nay. I'm braw." Lexi repeated her earlier words.

"Okay." He looked her up and down, and she went adorably pink again. Maybe she was too embarrassed to tell him the truth. "How did you lose your clothes? Did you go skinny-dipping or something?"

"Skinny…dipping?"

Graeme smirked. "You know, swimming naked?"

Lexi looked out toward the crashing waves before

meeting his eyes again. Those gorgeous almost-purple eyes stared up at him with leeriness that wasn't there before.

He didn't like it.

"A-aye."

He frowned. That was a lie.

Graeme could let it go for now, perhaps she was worried he'd judge her if she told him what'd really happened.

"Uh, okay. Well, let's go back to Dunvegan. Although, I do wonder where you've been. We've been working there two weeks; I sure would've noticed *you*. Even with clothes on." He winked, and she went even redder.

Damn if that little tidbit wasn't the truth. She had to be the hottest thing he'd seen since coming to Scotland, and he liked the crimson on her cheeks.

Not that the locals hadn't interested him. He wasn't a closeted virgin or anything, but other than admiring a girl or two from a distance on the occasional pub crawl, he hadn't bedded *any* Scottish beauty.

Bridget, who worked for Gramps, had shown interest in him, but he hadn't pursued the pretty redhead, either. Partly, so as to not piss off his grandfather, and partly because when he'd first come to Skye, he'd been staying with Gramps. Bringing anyone back there for a romp in the sack would've been awkward, at best. Inappropriate at the very least.

He had his own place now, not far from the office or his grandfather's house, but he'd been too busy, with work and Gramps' recovery to worry about Mr. Happy.

The old coot was still in physical therapy three days a week, of which Graeme had to force the man to go by driving him back and forth.

Lexi didn't answer, but she did follow him toward his borrowed pickup.

He opened the passenger door, but the young woman just stood there...staring at it.

Like she'd never seen a truck before.

"Coming?"

She scrambled forward, but her eyes were still saucers as she inspected the cab and tentatively touched the bench seat.

"Have you never ridden in a truck before?" Graeme asked.

She shot him a look before nodding. "Of course I have," she muttered in that attractive Highland brogue.

He frowned for the second time. Another lie?

"Do you need help up? It's high."

She was short, and Gramps didn't have running boards.

"Nay."

He got a full view of her delectable *bare* ass as Lexi got on all fours to climb into the truck. Would've laughed if he didn't think it would offend her.

This girl was gorgeous as hell, but she was...weird.

Sure, the Isle of Skye was kind of rural, but why would she lie about never riding in a pickup truck?

Surely the estate had vehicles other than the Beemer the current laird of place drove? The sleek black S-series was always out front when the guy was there.

Graeme had only met him twice, but Gramps had

known Mr. MacLeod for years.

He climbed behind the wheel and cranked the engine to life. "I'll never get used to driving on the wrong side of the car, the wrong side of the road," he muttered, more to himself than to Lexi.

She'd seemed to shrink away from him the more he spoke, and he didn't like it.

She drew her knees to her chest and wrapped her arms around herself on the charcoal gray-upholstered bench seat.

"You can't sit like that. You'll have to put your seatbelt on."

Lexi looked at him with sheer terror written all over her expression. Like she had no clue what he'd just said.

The loud diesel made the truck vibrate, and she swallowed again.

"Lexi?"

Her eyes shot to his.

Graeme leaned over, gently pried her hands away and helped her lower her tempting legs. He reached for the passenger belt, and drew it across her slender body. "It won't hurt you." When it snapped into place, he was reluctant to pull his hand away. "It's to keep you safe in your seat while I drive."

She didn't look comforted, and gnawed on her full bottom lip.

"Gimme a sec, and I'll grab a blanket so you can wrap it around you." He slid out of his seat and grabbed the rough woolen plaid from his grandfather's truck bed-toolbox.

He tossed it at Lexi when he got back in, but she left

the Clan MacDonald patterned tartan on her lap. Fright was still stamped on that beautiful face.

"Look, I don't know what's going on with you, but it *will* be okay. I'll keep you safe until we can figure out what happened. I'll keep you safe." Repeating himself seemed to be the theme of today, but Graeme wanted her to recognize the vow he'd just made.

Those eyes locked onto his, as if he was her lifeline, and a shudder wracked her small frame. She didn't speak or touch the blanket.

He leaned in and pressed his mouth to hers; couldn't help it.

The kiss was over before he could do what he really wanted to, taste her fully. He didn't want to freak her out more than she already was.

Graeme didn't take time to chide himself for giving in to the odd urge. He just wanted her to feel better. Not look so damn scared.

He made himself look away, and shoved the pickup into gear. "Let's go to Dunvegan."

chapter three

Whaddaya mean ye found her on the beach?"

Lexi watched, wrapped in the MacDonald plaid, as her rescuer spoke to an older man with a Highland brogue not unlike her own. She looked down at the dark reds and purples in the woven lines. So different than MacLeod colors. Her father would've frowned for sure.

Uncle Duncan would've had a snide remark. His wife's sister, Jules, was married to the Laird MacDonald, Hugh. The men always acted as if they hated each other, rooted in a a hundred-plus years old conflict, but they didn't really feel like that.

Peace had been found long ago, and Aunt Claire was close to her sister, and her niece, Brenna, who was a few summers younger than Lexi. They also lived on Skye, in the MacDonald stronghold, Armadale.

The older man speaking with Graeme was almost as tall him.

The handsome MacDonald, who'd put her in the strange conveyance was gesturing as he talked.

He kissed me.

Other than the press of her father's or her brother's lips to her cheek, it'd been the first time a man had kissed her.

The first time a man had put his mouth on hers.

It'd been so fleeting, but Lexi had *tasted* him, and that tiny sip had made her need more, as if she had an unquenchable thirst.

She'd watched his mouth the whole time he'd talked on the short ride—minutes that felt like hours because she'd been so scared. She'd clung to the door with one hand, and the other had been white-knuckled on the edge of the seat, until her fingers had lost sensation.

Even though it was a smoother ride than a horse and cart, she'd been so uncomfortable.

Graeme's deep voice had soothed—she couldn't help it; she'd fantasized about putting her lips to his again.

He'd called the thing a *truck*. Maybe it was like a car. So *that's* what Aunt Claire had talked about, but Lexi had always had trouble imagining them.

She shuddered. Preferred an open horseback ride.

Lexi stood next to the two men in the castle's courtyard that'd always been *home*.

She'd been able to recognize the place as Dunvegan, but it was so much different than the castle of 1694. There were no outer gates, no embattlement, and there was a flag on the top, as well as other slender items sticking up from roof. Maybe she could ask Graeme what they were. She'd never seen the like.

The castle structure itself was also different, but not so much that she couldn't see her home. However, she couldn't stop staring.

It was like something so important was missing, even though Claire had explained that their defensive way of life was much different than how the people lived in this time.

Her father, uncle and grandfather had been proud to learn their clan's legacy was still standing so far in the future, as her aunt had told them when she'd arrived in their time, before Lexi had been born.

Looking at it now, she could understand that sense, and wished her father and uncle, and also Aunt Janet, their sister — Liam's mother — could see it.

Perhaps her grandfather, who'd died a few years ago, knew *this* Dunvegan from heaven.

"People dinnae just appear from nowhere, lad. Not like Faeries."

She swallowed a gasp and focused on the man's face. Claire had told her people of the future didn't know of the Fae. Had her aunt been wrong?

The man had silver hair, shorn to his head, and his eyes were the same dark brown as Graeme's. His facial features marked them as kin, as if her rescuer would look the same as this man when older.

He'd mentioned his grandfather. This must be him. However, the elder MacDonald sounded like a Highlander, where the younger was all American — like Lila, Aunt Claire, and Aunt Jules.

Looking at him somehow made her miss her own grandfather. She'd enjoyed spending time with him, and her youngest cousin, Iain, had been named for him.

"She was on the beach, Gramps. Hasn't told me what happened. Not for lack of askin', really." Graeme's words were wrapped in exasperation, but instinct told her it wasn't pointed at her.

His grandfather looked at her harshly. She felt naked under his scrutiny, despite the gray leine and plaid wrapped around her like a skirt.

"Come, lassie, what do ye have ta say fer yerself?"

Lexi stepped closer, but when she opened her mouth, no words were born. Heat rushed her cheeks and she fought the urge to fidget.

"This one says yer name's MacLeod." The older man thumbed Graeme.

She forced a nod. "Aye, 'tis. I'm Alexandria MacLeod."

"Where do ye live?"

She looked at the castle throwing a huge shadow behind them. She couldn't tell them the exact truth. "I...grew up on Skye. Born and raised." She used the phrase Graeme had earlier, and threw him a nervous look.

When Lexi looked back at his grandfather, the man's bushy brows were furrowed, and he wore an impatient frown.

She wasn't the empath her mother was, but when someone was feeling a strong emotion, she could sometimes pick up on it.

He was displeased with her.

She was wasting his time, making him agitated.

Somehow that made her feel worse.

Lexi wanted to break their eye contact, but couldn't.

"How did you get to the beach?" Graeme's question was gentle, soft. Much the opposite of his grandfather's inquiries.

"I...dinnae remember." The lie fell from her lips.

"You don't remember? Like you hit your head?" Her rescuer asked, and she couldn't look away from his eyes.

"I dinnae ken." At least the delivery of the second lie was smoother.

"Do you think she has amnesia, Gramps?"

The old man's stare captured her attention again, and Lexi couldn't move.

It was like he could see right *through* her.

Like he could sense every untruth she'd ever uttered.

Worse than her mother.

"Are ye hurt, lassie?" he asked, the gruffness gone from his voice.

"I dinnae think so." She ordered herself to stand very still, as if he could slay her with a look were she to move.

The men peered at each other, then looked back at her again.

"I'll take her to the clinic. I think it's open. We drove by it this morning."

The older man nodded.

"I dinnae need a...physician." *Clinic* was a word she understood because Lila called her surgery at Dunvegan the same.

"I think it's a good idea to be safe," Graeme insisted.

"Indeed," his grandfather agreed.

"I..."

"If you can't remember anything, darlin', that's a

problem." Her rescuer's voice was that baby soft hum again, and if it'd come from anyone else, it would've roused her ire.

Like when her father talked to her as if she was still a wee lassie. From this man, Graeme, it made her tummy wobble and her face heat. Not from embarrassment, but because he didn't know her, yet he cared about her.

Why did someone she didn't know have this effect on her?

Lexi cleared her throat. "O-o-okay." She forced Aunt Claire's word out, because she needed to fit in here, and she'd already shown her uncertainty about several things; first Graeme's leine, then the truck. Best not to give them anything more to believe she didn't belong exactly in this time period.

Nor could she reveal her terror at the idea of a doctor other than her sister-by-marriage examining her, which would make them doubt her further.

She hollered at herself to calm.

Simply looking her over in an exam couldn't betray the fact she'd time-traveled. Yet she needed to keep that truth a secret for now.

Lexi wouldn't volunteer that information to anyone, including the handsome MacDonald.

The gray cotton still swallowed the woman like a tent, even though Graeme had helped her fasten the blanket around her waist so it looked like a long kilt and he'd rolled the sleeves of his shirt.

He'd grabbed another shirt for himself, but the long-sleeved flannel was too warm, and he'd borrowed it from Gramps. It was all he could do on such short notice, but he was already sweating.

He had a sudden sense of urgency regarding getting Lexi to the clinic, but it wasn't like there was a magic cure for amnesia.

Why hadn't he thought of that before?

The assumed-condition connected so many dots about her odd behavior.

Graeme considered giving her something else to wear, but he didn't want to wait to take her to a doctor. Besides, he didn't have any clothing handy that would fit her. Later he'd take her to the nearest store in Armadale and let her pick her own clothes.

For now, the blanket and shirt covered all her pertinent parts, which was *not* a wholly awesome thing. Lexi wore *naked* quite beautifully. It was a shame to cover such gorgeous real estate.

He spared her a glance and rebuked the dirty thoughts.

She crouched her body into a small ball on the seat, like she'd done the first time he'd put her in his grandfather's truck. Vulnerable and tiny.

Guilt took a bite out of him.

He really was a sleaze.

"You really don't like trucks, do you?"

"All is well." Her voice belied her words. They shook as much as the tremor wracking her slender shoulders.

He put his hand on her thigh and squeezed. Cursed

the blanket to hell, because he'd rather be touching her soft bare skin, like before. "It's not far, I promise."

"I dinnae need a physician," she whispered, repeating the sentiment from earlier, but at least she was looking at him.

"Well, if you hit your head, you need to get checked out. Trust me, it's for the best."

Lexi touched her forehead and the crown of her ebony hair. "I dinnae feel any...injury."

"Maybe it's something you *can't* feel. Or hell, maybe there's another reason for your amnesia. What's the last thing you remember? Do you know how long you were on the beach or how you got there?" He flexed his grip on the steering wheel, then pulled onto the road.

She closed her eyes and shook her head, making that dark curtain sway. "I...dinnae know."

"See?" Graeme frowned. "All the more reason to get you checked out."

"Thank ye."

Her voice was so low he almost missed it.

He smiled. "You're welcome. Anytime."

The feel of her lips under his danced into his memories. Even though that kiss had been tiny, he'd never experienced such a soft, delicious mouth. He wanted to kiss her again, right then and not *stop* kissing her.

Do way more than kiss her, considering he'd seen all her goods. Felt her perfect breasts against his bare chest.

His dick liked his train of thought and stirred.

What the hell?

Sure, one would naturally feel sympathy and worry for someone found in peril, but his...desire...for this quirky foundling female was strange. The strength of his need was even more concerning.

Graeme needed to get a grip.

He shifted on the seat in lieu of grabbing his crotch for a much-needed adjustment. He'd have to do it when they got to the clinic, and be subtle about it.

He cleared his throat. "Do you know where you are?"

Lexi had scanned the length of the road as they drove down the winding two-lane road. She glanced at him; confusion written all over her pretty face. "'Tis different, but dinnae be all tha' different by the same."

"What d'you mean?"

Her cheeks went crimson and she resumed her studies out the passenger window.

She didn't answer.

Graeme watched her for a few seconds before forcing his eyes back on the road.

She squirmed, as if she was uncomfortable.

What had she meant?

He narrowed his eyes as he appraised her again.

Was she being dishonest about something?

Don't be an ass. She doesn't remember anything. She's not lying. But...

She'd lied about riding in a truck before. Hadn't she?

Or was it just she didn't remember *that*, either?

Amnesia wouldn't make her forget general, *normal* things, would it?

She'd remembered...recognized...Dunvegan the first time Graeme had mentioned it, hadn't she?

He considered her profile and shook his head. Pressing her further wouldn't work.

When he'd fired questions at her a few minutes ago, her eyes had gone misty, and he wouldn't be the asshat who made her cry.

Stress might even have a more negative effect, and make things worse, but what the hell did he know? He wasn't a doctor.

Lexi continued to *not* answer his last inquiry about her puzzling statement.

Graeme concentrated on the narrow roadway.

The clinic was just up head. He might not be a doctor, but hopefully one there could help them figure things the hell out.

chapter four

The anesthetic hospitaly-clinicy smell hit his senses, but he didn't want to take his focus off the beautiful enigma he'd found on the beach.

She was perched on the narrow examination table, sitting on top of the standard crinkly thin white paper, and she looked terrified and tiny.

Again.

Graeme didn't like it.

Every time Lexi moved, even slightly, the paper screamed, and she'd shudder a little. It only got worse when Dr. Guinn approached.

Somehow that made his gut ache.

The young doctor circled the table, muttering unintelligible things under his breath. He couldn't be much older than Graeme, but he had a trimmed goatee a few shades darker than his light brown hair, probably grown purposely to make him appear older.

He wasn't very tall, and he had a face that immediately felt trustworthy. He wore Harry Potter-esque glasses, but his brown eyes were kind. He had the complete look of a caring medical professional.

However, all those things seemed to fail to put the patient at ease.

Graeme wanted to glare. Or bark at the man to say

something to *them*, instead of himself.

The more he didn't address them, the more Lexi shied away from the stethoscope, but the perk was she inched closer to *him*.

He must've reassured her a hundred times, which had evidently meant nothing. When they'd arrived and she'd learned the doctor was male, her pretty violet eyes had grown to the size of dinner plates. She'd squeezed his hand, and insisted he go into the exam room with her.

Not that he minded, but the nurse had.

Even now, the petite brunette glared at him over her clipboard, leaning on the counter while Doc Guinn did his thing.

Lexi's fidgets made the wrinkled disposable sheet under her perfect bottom rattle, and she shot him another uncertain glance.

"Take a deep breath for me." The doctor's refined English accent snagged Graeme's attention, but he threw a reassuring smile at his charge.

The stethoscope was on her supple flesh, up under the fabric of his tee, and she looked like she was about to jump out of her skin.

The blanket was still covering her legs, but the doctor had moved it down, so he could palpate her belly.

That—along with urging her to lie back—hadn't gone so well; Lexi's limbs had trembled so hard Graeme feared he'd lose his grip on her fingers.

He'd entwined them with his then, and started making soothing circles on the back of her hand with his thumb.

She'd only calmed a little.

"It's okay, Lexi darlin', just do what he says." He tried to keep his voice low and even.

She locked onto his eyes, her pretty face so frantic he wanted to yank her off the table and hold her close, then carry her out of the place, as if the doctor had assaulted her.

"He's almost done." Graeme arched an eyebrow in the man's direction, to ensure his words were true. Or at least encourage the good doc to hurry the hell up.

Guinn cleared his throat. "Ah, yes, I'm almost through." He straightened the gray shirt, and patted Lexi's back.

Instead of taking reassurance from the small touch, she jerked away, again, closer to Graeme. If he'd been sitting next to her instead of standing, no doubt she would've been in his lap.

It took all he was made of not to slip his arm around her shoulders. Holding her hand, stroking her clammy fingers wasn't enough.

His gaze brushed the nurse's, and she narrowed her eyes, her disapproval a live thing.

Just because they weren't married didn't mean Graeme didn't have a place at her side. Unfortunately, he couldn't convince the Scottish version of Nurse Ratchet of such.

"She doesn't appear to have a concussion. Let's check your reflexes, and maybe we'll get a better picture," the doctor said.

The look Lexi shot Graeme was pure fright, all semblance of that tiny sense of peace gone.

He took a step closer to the exam table; couldn't help

that any more than the kiss on her hand moments before. "Shhh, darlin' it's okay. It doesn't hurt."

She took a big breath, and despite his oversized shirt on her, her breasts heaved, and spun him into more memories he needed to banish already.

Doc Guinn did his thing with the little reflex hammer, although Lexi tensed and had to be told to relax a few times when he moved the blanket and bared the length of her shapely legs.

Damn, they were sexy, and quite long, despite her slight height of five feet three inches—confirmed by Scottish Nurse Ratchet when she'd taken Lexi's vitals.

Of course, he'd had to ask how many feet 1.61 meters was, but whatever. He was getting used to the metric system. He'd trained with it in college, but his practical application was a since-Scotland thing.

"Well, I do not see anything physically wrong, to be honest, Mr., em, MacDonald." The man's brown eyes were concerned, as he peered down at his patient again, barely sparing a glimpse at Graeme, despite the address. "You do not have any pain, aye, Miss MacLeod?"

Hearing the Scottish affirmative in the English accent didn't sound right—different from what he usually heard on Skye—although it was common enough.

Lexi looked at him before regarding the doctor again, and shook her head, making her dark locks scatter.

She swallowed and Graeme wanted to press his lips to the tender spot on her neck. Not for the first time that day.

The nurse's pen darted across the paper on her clipboard as the doctor spoke.

"Can you tell me again what happened today?" he asked.

When they'd arrived, Graeme had given the nurse—then the doctor—a rundown of finding Lexi on the beach, leaving out the *naked* part. He'd explained that she didn't know how she'd gotten there. He didn't want the medical staff to think she needed a psych ward, so he also left out her aversion to the pickup truck, as well as her weird comments about the terrain.

Dr. Guinn had asked her questions about her childhood, apparently testing her long-term memory, and even though her voice had been low and hesitant, Lexi had answered each one, proving she remembered some things about her life.

The closer the inquires got to that morning, the fuzzier she seemed to get, but she knew her name, how old she was—twenty-one—and didn't *that* make him feel like an asshole for wanting her.

She might look *all* woman, but she was young. Too young to be the star of Graeme's new fantasies. He *shouldn't* have kissed her. She wasn't a kid, but she was closer to one than not.

Not like thirty made him an old man, but he was too old for her, wasn't he?

His dick didn't like that idea, for sure.

He would've never guessed she was only twenty-one. She looked older—mid-twenties had been his original ballpark.

He'd wanted to demand, "are you sure?" when

she'd revealed her age to Dr. Guinn.

A memory of the gorgeous acreage of her bare flesh danced into his brain, confirming—or contradicting—the notion she wasn't fit for his...what? His want, his desires? He had a good damn imagination.

Lexi's, uh, assets certainly didn't shout *child*.

You're still a perv...

Graeme told his conscience to go to hell. Now wasn't the time for any of that, anyway. They needed to figure her out.

"Well, it's encouraging that you remember some history about your life, both long-term and recent," the doctor said, wearing a contemplative expression. He stroked his goatee with his thumb and forefinger.

Lexi looked at Graeme again, and he brought their joined hands to his mouth, pressing his lips to her knuckles, like he'd done it before.

Like it was the most natural thing in the world.

The light curve of her luscious smile kicked his heart into overdrive, but at least she seemed to have calmed a bit.

"I could order an MRI. Since there's no obvious injury or evidence Ms. MacLeod bumped her head, it might help us determine another cause. Brain damage or evidence of seizures."

"Seizure?" she asked. She struggled with the word, as if it was unfamiliar.

After a brief explanation, Lexi affirmed she'd never had one.

He added that bit of knowledge to his, *this chick is weird* list. How could she not know what a seizure was?

The amnesia was worse than Doc Guinn thought?

"An MRI?" Graeme asked. "Is that necessary?"

If Lexi couldn't handle a ride in a pickup truck, she'd never be able to tolerate the close quarters and noise of an MRI machine.

They'd need a white jacket for sure.

The doctor took one last hard look at his patient before meeting Graeme's eyes. "Her memories could come back on their own. Since we don't know the cause, we can't determine how severe her case is. There are several different types of amnesia."

So, the doctor agreed with Graeme and his grandfather's assumption.

"It may be prudent to see if the situation sorts itself." Dr. Guinn offered a small reassuring smile.

"That's possible?" he asked.

Scottish Nurse Ratchet shot him a death look, as if she was at her wits end with the two men going back and forth on Lexi's behalf, instead of the patient speaking for herself.

"Oh, aye. Taking her around familiar things could be a good start."

Graeme nodded and squeezed Lexi's fingers, choosing not to remind the doctor they'd met that morning. Besides Dunvegan, what was familiar for his little charge?

She'd said she was born and raised on Skye.

"I can totally do that," he said, throwing a wink at Lexi when he felt her eyes on him.

Perhaps she was wondering how, too, since they didn't know each other, but she didn't throw him under the bus to the doctor, either.

"Do you remember where you live?" Doc Guinn asked, peering at his patient again.

She startled on the table, and inadvertently tugged on Graeme's hand.

"Is that a no?" the doctor asked, his brows dipping in concern.

Lexi visibly hesitated, then shrugged one shoulder, but didn't speak.

"What about people?" he continued, as if she hadn't *not* answered.

"Graeme. His grandfa."

Graeme arched an eyebrow and stared, even as his name in her tempting brogue rolled over him just like earlier.

"They're the only people you know? Do you remember any of your family or where they might live?"

She shook her head, but it also held that same hesitation.

His curiosity peaked. His gut coughed up an accusation.

She's lying.

No. She couldn't be.

She has amnesia.

The doctor had confirmed it.

Then why…

Graeme shut down his negative thoughts. Lexi couldn't be lying. She hadn't mentioned Dunvegan to the doctor, but maybe she hadn't *really* recognized it when he'd said it on the beach. Maybe it just seemed as if she had?

He could remind her she'd said she'd been born and raised on the Isle of Skye, but he held his tongue. That was a better conversation for when they were back in the truck again. *Alone.* He refused to let his suspicions about possible dishonesty dance around in his head anymore.

She was sweet, lost, and…innocent.

He was compelled to help her.

Why would she lie, anyway?

Could someone with amnesia be intentionally dishonest?

Maybe he should ask Doc Guinn, but he didn't want to.

The more he watched her, the more she struggled with the doctor's new round of questions, the more Graeme wanted to shout, "We're done here." Sweep her up in his arms and flee.

Protect her.

Lexi was becoming visibly upset, and he wanted it all to stop. She was making herself small again, like she'd done in the truck. Terror was written all over her pretty face.

He managed to only politely clear his throat, after squeezing her hand for another round of reassurance. "When do we come back, if her memories don't return?"

The doctor reclined on his stool, and stroked his goatee like he'd done before. "Two weeks?" He exchanged a glance with Scottish Nurse Ratchet, and she nodded.

Guinn's brown gaze swept over Lexi, but landed on Graeme. "However, if there are any changes, please bring her back straightaway. Nausea, vomiting, loss of appetite or dizziness. Any improvement or deterioration of her condition. But let's hope for the best."

"You got it, doc." He looked at his little enigma, and offered a smile he wished would give her some measure of comfort, since touch alone didn't seem to be helping.

Those big, luminous violet eyes blinked back, but her shoulders loosened a little.

Graeme would take what he could get.

For now.

chapter five

exi tamped down panic and dread, taking Graeme's hand as soon as her feet touched the floor of the exam room.

The physician hadn't hurt her, and his brown eyes were kind, but she hadn't wanted him to touch her.

Then the questions...they made her head spin.

How could she continue to pretend she'd lost her memories?

She glanced at the man who'd rescued her. He was so kind and handsome.

How could she...lie to him?

Nay, how can I tell him the truth?

Graeme would think her mad.

She could make it all stop. She could flee to the beach, open the Faery Stones and go home.

Lexi didn't want to.

She wasn't ready to face her family, especially her mother. That same guilt from before floated up from her belly, and she pushed it back down. They would be worried sick, but she couldn't be concerned with them now. Right?

What she knew of what her Aunt Claire had called "modern times" was that magic was diminished, so would hers even work?

She could try.

She *really* didn't want to.

The doctor and nurse exchanged some more words with Graeme, and the nurse's concerned blue eyes landed on her.

Lexi mustered a smile, but she really just wanted to cling to her rescuer.

The older woman smiled back, but her stare was still assessing.

She wanted to squirm.

"C'mon, darlin', let's go." He put his hand on the small of her back, urging her to take a few steps toward the door.

Lexi liked the warm feeling above her bottom, through the thick fabric of the plaid he'd given her. She'd re-tucked it around her waist, and it caressed her thighs as she walked.

His palm was so warm, it made her yearn for his hands to be on her bare body.

Anywhere.

Graeme led them out to his blue truck.

Her stomach churned at the idea of getting back inside it, despite the fact her two rides had been smooth.

"Hang on a minute, okay?" he said, his hand on the door.

Lexi nodded, and took a breath of relief that they weren't rushing back into the conveyance.

He pulled a black, flat rectangular item from his back pocket and touched it in a few places. Then he put the thing to his ear.

She cocked her head to one side.

What was that thing? What was he doing?

If Lexi asked, Graeme would surely assume something was wrong with her—worse than missing memories.

"Hey, Bridget."

She startled.

A female voice came *out* of the black thing.

Graeme turned his back to her, so Lexi inched closer, trying to learn—hear—more.

A combination of fear and curiosity churned the butterflies in her tummy.

Maybe there was magic in this time, after all?

"Are you at the office?" Graeme asked.

He paused and the woman said something she couldn't make out.

Lexi wanted to get even closer, but she was practically touching him, as it was.

"Oh, okay, no problem." Her rescuer said into the black thing. "No, no, Gramps is fine. Uh, where would you take a woman to buy clothes? Local, without driving all the way back to Armadale or Calligarry? Unless—"

The female voice sounded again, and again, Lexi couldn't make out the words, but the woman sounded wary—or something else.

A sense of unease prickled beneath the surface of her skin.

Who was this woman to Graeme?

He laughed with a hesitant, nervous edge. "Well, it's a long story. Yeah, I'll tell you later. Can you help me out?"

Lexi frowned.

The woman made some kind of loud exclamation, then cursed in Gaelic.

That, she understood. She smirked, then pulled her mouth down at the corners.

Why was the woman cursing at Graeme's question?

That odd sensation hit her again, and she curled her lip. Wanted to demand who the woman was.

"Okay, thank you, Bridget. Means a lot to me, seriously." The black thing made a sound, and he slid it in his back into his pocket.

Graeme whirled—and almost knocked her over.

She wobbled on her feet.

"Whoa!" His hand shot out and steadied her for what seemed the tenth time that day. "You were pretty much on top me of me. Were you eavesdropping?" There was a playful curve to his delectable mouth.

On top of him?

Heat seared Lexi's cheeks and her gaze shot to the ground.

"Hey, I'm not mad." Graeme's thick fingers urged her chin up, and their eyes met.

She swallowed and forced a nod. "I—"

"No worries, really."

He flashed an easy smile that did things to her insides.

"Sorry," she pushed out.

"Bridget works for Gramps," he said, as if she'd asked—or as if he'd read her mind. "Just thought she could help, and she did. Let's go get you some clothes. So you don't have to stay wrapped in that blanket or swim in my shirt all day."

Lexi grabbed the sleeve of the odd gray leine. It was as soft as some of the fine fabrics her mother always ordered from the dressmaker. "I like this...shirt."

Graeme's smile widened, and the flutter in her belly kicked up a few notches.

"And I like my shirt on you, too. But we probably should get you some proper underwear, and uh...stuff." He looked away, and shoved his hands through his sandy hair.

She could always use the shrinking spell to make it fit—if it would even work, but he was probably right. She needed some proper clothing actually made for a lass. Faked memory loss would only get her so far.

You could go home.

The very unwelcome whisper was so reminiscent of her mother, she fought a wince. She made tight fists at her sides.

"Are you okay?" Graeme's voice was coated in concern, and he invaded her personal space. "You sure you're not in pain?"

"Nay." She shook her head for effect. "Why?"

"You...uh...winced or something. I know Doc Guinn said you don't look like you hit your head but are you really sure?" His hands landed on her shoulders.

Lexi wanted to move closer, bask in the body heat, but she instead forced another nod and chided herself to stay where she was. "I'm braw."

He cocked an eyebrow, but after several moments of scrutiny, he nodded. "I'll just have to believe you, I guess."

Guilt swirled around again, but she ignored it, and

let him help her into the truck.

"We're not going far," Graeme said when he cranked the thing to life.

She jumped from the noise and the vibration under her bottom.

"Seatbelt, okay?" He reached over, but she raised a hand.

"I can do it." She'd seen him take the strap, move it across her body and plug it into what looked like a metal narrow hole-like thing.

She needed to show him she wasn't mad—or helpless. She'd never blend into this time if she stayed so afraid of her surroundings.

Lexi was a MacLeod, for *Jesusakes*, as her Uncle Duncan would say.

She grabbed the seatbelt and had to pull harder than expected. It slipped from her grip and slammed into the door with a loud *knock*.

Lexi squealed.

Her rescuer chuckled.

She huffed, and threw him a small glare. "I can do it," she repeated, like when her little cousin Iain was being petulant. She took a subtle breath and tried again, this time holding more firmly and drawing the strap across her torso.

A *click* reverberated in the truck, and a sense of satisfaction rushed over her.

Lexi had done something for herself—even if tiny.

What Graeme had called a seatbelt was made of what looked like a thick-ridged ribbon, and she liked how it felt. She rubbed her fingertips back and forth.

He watched her from the corner of his eye, but didn't say anything as the truck moved onto the road.

She didn't miss his smile, though.

Somehow, that made Lexi smile, too.

Graeme was the dumbest man on Earth — or at least on the Isle of Skye.

The only thing he knew about women's clothing was taking them off. Err, well he'd had years of that during and after college. With as lost as Lexi seemed, how was *he* supposed to be the one to help her find appropriate clothing?

Bridget had grudgingly given him the name of two small boutiques that were close, still in Dunvegan. They were down the road a ways, but it was better than the trek back to Armadale, which was over an hour's drive.

Maybe he should've taken his little charge back to Armadale and enlisted Bridget's help to clothe her.

Then again, Gramps' assistant had seemed so suspicious with just minor questions. God knew what she would've said to, "Yeah, I did actually find a strange woman naked on the beach."

His gut said the distrusting redhead wouldn't like Lexi from origin story alone.

However, she only needed the basics, so Graeme would have to make do, although he wasn't convinced he'd find her a proper bra and panties set if the place was only offering homemade wares.

Lexi had looked up at him with those guileless

violet eyes and told him she liked his shirt on her body.

Damn, he did, too.

Or better yet, her out of it.

Lying in a pile on the floor next to his bed.

Stop it.

Graeme pulled the truck into a tiny parking space.

The small stand-alone building was cute, and it didn't look much different than the cottage he was staying at in Calligarry.

He'd rented the place to get out of his grumpy grandfather's house, and like this one appeared to be, it was over one hundred years old—maybe two hundred.

A hand-painted sign hung from the awning. *Flora's Fashions*, in white lettering with pink flowers, along with the Gaelic lettering of what he assumed was the same beneath it.

According to Bridget, her mother's friend, Flora Nicholson, owned the place, and had for the past thirty odd years.

Graeme helped Lexi out of the truck, but she shut the door.

It was the first time she'd touched it, and damn if she didn't look proud of herself.

He couldn't help but smile.

"A crofter's cottage?" she asked as she glanced at Flora's little shop.

"What?"

"Ah…" Lexi shook her head.

"It's a clothing store."

She opened her mouth, but snapped it closed so fast he worried for her teeth.

"C'mon," he said, offering a smile to make her feel better.

There was an antique-looking cow bell on the top of the door, and they looked up collectively when it *dinged*.

Lexi smiled, as if it was something she recognized, but Graeme didn't ask, because an older woman with a full head of fluffy gray hair and bright red glasses tipped on her nose came toward them.

"Helllllllo, dearies," she said, as if she'd stepped right out of that old movie, *Mrs. Doubtfire*.

"Hey," Graeme said. "We, uh, need some clothes for my…friend." He shoved his hands in his jeans' pockets and looked around.

The place seemed larger than from the outside, and there were hanging racks of clothing and shelving covering the perimeter walls, as well as four or five round racks surrounding them. In the middle of all of it was an old-fashioned glass-topped counter with an ancient cash register sitting on the far left.

It smelled nice, as if Flora had embraced her name and pumped floral essence in the air.

"Aye, I see can see that." She closed the distance between them, and took Lexi's hands. "Och, dearie what happened to ye?" Her accent was a tad more refined than his grandfather's, but he still sounded like a local.

"I…"

"Dinnae say it, dearie," the shopkeeper tsked and threw him a dark look. "This'in dinnae hurt ye?" She dropped her voice, but it was a stage-whisper.

Graeme bristled, but Lexi beat him to speaking.

"Graeme has been takin' good care a' me."

Mrs. Doubtfire turned into Cruella Deville as she eyed him up and down.

He wanted to roll his eyes, but remained still under her scrutiny.

"Graeme, is it?" Flora asked, without releasing Lexi's hands. His name rolled off her tongue in the attractive Highlander brogue, but it was more like spitting a curse.

He frowned. This woman didn't know him.

"It is." He cleared his throat. "Graeme MacDonald. James MacDonald is my grandfather, and we're working at the big house. This is Lexi, and she needs some help."

She visibly softened at the mention of Gramps. "The American grandson."

Graeme nodded.

"Flora Nicholson." She threw her hand out for a shake.

He really wanted to roll his eyes now. Of course, mentioning the grumpy codger would make her nicer to him. Everyone *loved* his grandfather. He just didn't want too many questions asked about Lexi.

"I've known yer grandfather for eons."

Of course, she has.

He nodded.

"Well then, lassie, let's get ye fixed up." Flora threw him a glare. Cruella was back. "Ye, stay here."

chapter six

exi's eyes drank up all the fabric before her. She'd never seen so many garments in her life, not even the time her family had traveled to Edinburgh, where there had been several dress shops.

She wanted to run through the small place, arms spread, touching everything. Colors swam before her vision; bright ones, pastels, white, black, stripes, prints. Patterns she'd never seen before, materials that looked like they'd been conjured.

"So many…" Lexi whispered.

Flora Nicholson must be the most talented dressmaker ever to exist. Did she have magic?

She reached for a pink leine, not unlike the oversized gray one she was wearing. It was so soft, maybe even more so than Graeme's.

"Like that, do ye?" the older woman asked. "Take it, we'll try it on ye."

"How did you make them all?" she blurted.

Flora gave a hearty laugh. "I dinnae, lassie. I make some dresses, aye, but most are shipped in. From designers and suppliers." She gestured to a pretty flowered frock hanging on a wooden figure shaped like a person.

Lexi's cheeks burned. She couldn't muster words, so

she looked away from the older woman's kind, keen green eyes.

She needed to fit in to this time, so she needed to stop blurting foolish things to make it more obvious she wasn't quite when she belonged.

The shop owner was watching her silently.

She fought the urge to squirm for the thousandth time that very odd day.

"Lassie?"

Lexi forced a smile and cleared her throat. "I'm braw."

Flora cocked her head to one side. "Aye."

She wanted to flee to Graeme's side. She couldn't see him, since the older woman had taken her to the back of the crofter's cabin-turned marketplace, but Lexi could sense him.

He watched her from afar — or at least that's what her instincts whispered.

"Come, dearie, I have a few underthings I think ye need."

She followed the older woman into the farthest recesses of the small building; behind a dark green curtain. It looked like a storage area, because there were brown trunk or chest-like squares of several sizes, some open and some appearing to be sealed shut. They were stacked against the far wall, as well as on top of each other.

Flora grabbed one and started rifling through it. It was a container of sorts, but it didn't seem sturdy like the wooden crates she'd seen in the deep stores of Dunvegan. It had a flap that moved back and forth as the older woman kept searching for something.

"Ah, here. This should fit ye." She handed Lexi something in a see-through package that made a crinkling noise when handled.

She liked the sound and held the thing against her torso, moving her fingers back and forth over it, so it would make the sound again. She smiled and met Flora's eyes.

The older woman had an eyebrow arched. "Open it, dearie."

Again, Lexi's cheeks scorched. She held the thing up. Inside was a something purple with little dots that were a darker purple printed on it. A scrap of fabric?

She didn't know what she held in her hands, and she couldn't ask.

"Dearie? Yer lookin' at those knickers like you've never seen the like before. Are you well?"

Knickers?

"A-aye," she forced out. Her face was probably bright red. Even her ears burned. She managed to rip the clear package and take out the purple knickers.

The material was soft and stretchy, and it had lace along the edges. It was pretty. If it was a garment, where and how was it worn?

Of course, Lexi couldn't ask, so she stood there, holding the item, and thankfully, Flora turned away, looking in another brown square.

"I'm sure I have a few brassieres around here. Ye dinnae have much, I dinnae think, but ye need support. No proper lady can run 'round without one."

She cocked her head to one side. She'd heard her

aunts refer to something called a *bra*, but she'd never seen one. They'd described it as some sort of corset.

Lexi struggled to remember, wishing she'd paid better attention to the "future talk" her Aunt Claire and sister-by-marriage, Lila, shared.

"Ah, here we are! I knew I had a few. Dinnae sell them, really, but I'm glad I dinnae toss them to the rubbish!" The shopkeeper smiled as she straightened. The white, lacy thing in her hands looked like the upper part of a bodice, without any stays attached.

From the shape, she assumed it would cradle her breasts.

Why?

What had the shopkeeper meant, Lexi didn't have much? Much of what?

She cocked her head to one side, but didn't voice the questions pushing against her lips. She had to appear to fit in to this time.

Flora held up the piece of clothing against Lexi's chest. "Aye, this should do it." She smiled, and their eyes met. "I'll grab some stockings, and we'll get ye dressed, dearie."

Lexi nodded because she couldn't say anything she was thinking.

The first thing she tried on was the soft pink leine. She loved the way it felt against her skin, but somehow regretted Graeme's gray one lying in a pile on the floor.

This one fit nicely, as it should, and fell to her waist.

Flora hadn't left the curtained area, but she was offering Lexi some privacy by turning away.

She didn't mind, but she didn't know how to don all

the things the older woman wanted her to try on, and she couldn't exactly ask. She dropped the plaid, the garment pooling at her feet.

"I like this," Lexi said, petting the fabric over her breasts and stomach.

The shopkeeper whirled to face her. "Och, lass! Ye dinnae put on the knickers!" She glanced at the chair with the pile of clothes. "Or the brassiere?"

Lexi's face burned and she looked down. She was embarrassed, but she also didn't understand the reproach in Flora's voice.

"Poor dearie. Dinnae fash. I'll help ye."

Her heart skipped a beat, but she didn't shy away from the older woman when she grabbed the small purple material and shook it out.

Flora knelt down, holding the knickers out and open. "Here, step into these."

Lexi cocked her head, and gingerly put her hand on the woman's shoulder, so she wouldn't lose her balance. She obeyed and put one foot in each hole.

When her companion straightened, she arched a bushy eyebrow again. "What're ye waitin' fer? Pull 'em up."

She startled, but again, followed the instructions and pulled the stretchy fabric over her thighs until it cupped her bottom and covered her most private parts. Lexi wiggled. She'd never worn anything so close. It was like a hug.

A loin cloth of sorts, perhaps?

Flora watched her, and she muttered something about knickers under her breath, but her keen gaze made

Lexi want to squirm. "Glad they fit ye. I assume ye need more, and I have a few pairs the same size. Now, get that shirt off so we can get the bra on ye, then we'll have ye dressed proper."

She nodded and pulled the pink leine over her head.

Flora grabbed the bra off the chair. "Arms out, I'll help ye with this, too."

Lexi nodded and did as bid, praying the older woman didn't think her mad, despite helping her dress.

Graeme gulped. He was so screwed. His mouth went dry, his tongue glued to the roof of his mouth.

Lexi twirled in the dark skinny jeans that clung to the curve of her perfect—oh, so perfect—ass and hips.

They were painted on and revealed so much, despite the modest cut and semi-high waist. She was more decently covered than she'd been all day, yet she'd never been so attractive.

Well, except when she'd been naked, but he was still trying to—unsuccessfully—banish that picture from his brain.

She was so damn sexy in a simple V-neck baby pink tee that also looked as if it'd been made just for her.

She's twenty-one years old.

Twenty-one is an adult.

There was no use standing there arguing with himself. He took a subtle breath and pushed off the old glass counter. It creaked a protest, and he cursed himself to Hades.

Flora must've found her a bra, because she was obviously wearing one.

Lexi's breasts weren't huge, but not tiny, either — another thing he'd not likely forget, any time soon, and they appeared higher, supported, under the pink cotton.

"Ye like?" Lexi asked, twirling again, as if she was dressed in a ballgown and not in a T-shirt and tight denim.

She wiggled her bare toes, and even that was damn cute. Her long dark hair surrounded her like curtains, and yet it was smoother, more ordered. Flora must've put a brush to it.

Graeme cleared his throat. "Y-y-yeah, you look great." Better than he could've imagined. Her ass was made for clingy jeans.

She petted her thighs in a downward motion, as if she'd never felt denim before. "I like these trews verra much."

Trews?

What the hell were trews?

He threw a glance at Flora, but the shopkeeper watched silently, as if assessing.

"Are ye settled, then, lassie? Ye dinnae want a skirt?"

Lexi shook her head. "I've always preferred trews to skirts, but my mother —" She snapped her mouth closed, and her face went bright pink.

Graeme took a step forward. "Your mother? Do you remember something, Lexi?" His heart tripped over the next few beats.

She tilted her head to one side and that little pink

tongue darted out, moistening her lips. Her chest heaved with a deep breath. "I—" She averted her gaze, and shook her head. When Lexi looked back at him, she shrugged. "I dinnae."

Flora patted her hand. "Dinnae force it, dearie. 'Twill come with time."

His little charge seemed to relax at the touch, and she gave a slight nod.

She must've told the shopkeeper she'd lost her memory when they'd been in the back, because Graeme hadn't said a word.

Since they'd come from behind the green curtain, Flora looked at Graeme a little kinder.

He snorted. Maybe "the American grandson" wasn't so bad after all?

Someone should tell Gramps that.

Flora handed him two large paper bags with woven handles. "Here, lad. These are for her."

He glanced down, and although he couldn't make out individual items, the bags were heavy, full to the brim with clothes. He spotted a few pairs of panties, new in the packages, and some socks.

Lexi had modeled a few things she'd tried on, wearing a huge grin that'd made his heart stutter, but what was in the bags had to be way more than two dresses, a pair of capris and one other pair of jeans.

"How much do I owe you?" Graeme asked. He set one down at his feet and reached for his wallet.

Flora shook her head and gestured with both hands. "No, no, I'll no' have it."

"But—"

"No, lad. I dinnae turn those away in need. The lassie was in need, and 'tis my pleasure to help."

"Wow. Thanks. I mean it." Graeme smiled and hefted each bag.

Lexi threw her arms around Flora, and the older woman gathered her up in a grandmotherly hug.

"Any time, dearie. If ye need anathin', do come back an' see me."

His little charge's smile was wide, genuine, and beautiful. "Thank ye," she whispered a few times. She also whispered something in Gaelic, and the older woman nodded.

Gaelic.

Another thing she hadn't forgotten. He filed it away, as another oddity about the girl he'd found on the beach.

When they got back in the truck, Lexi belted herself in the seat, again. "Thank ye, Graeme."

He squeezed the steering wheel with both hands until his knuckles were white and smarted, because the way his name rolled off her tongue in that brogue made him want to caress her cheek.

"Where're we goin?" she asked when he pulled onto the road.

"Uh, home, I guess?" Graeme swallowed. Pictured Lexi laying in his bed in his small Calligarry cottage, her new clothing covering the floor of his small bedroom.

I'm in so much trouble.

chapter seven

raeme had pulled out the black rectangle again and used it as they got in the truck.

Lexi's fascination hadn't dimmed, especially when he'd told her he had to "call" his grandfather. Call him what? And the man wasn't anywhere around to talk to. She'd openly stared in his direction as he yet again spoke into the black object.

The elder MacDonald had told him to take her back to Calligarry, and stated he would see them both the next morning. His gravelly voice had come *out* of the box. At first, she hadn't been able to hear him, but her rescuer had touched the box and it was louder, allowing her to hear him speak.

Was it magic?

Graeme had looked upset when their conversation had ended, and her heart skipped for him.

The bags of clothing rested between them, and she wished they were not there, so she could move closer to him.

"Are ye well?" she asked.

He glanced at her, and their eyes locked for a few moments, as he turned onto a different road. "Oh yeah. No worries. Gramps and I just— Well, we don't always get along."

"Why?"

He chuckled, but it didn't sound as if he was truly amused. "I don't want to bog you down with my sob story. You have enough to deal with, losing your memory and all."

Lexi glanced down at her lap when guilt jumped up from her tummy. She was lying to him, and she didn't like it.

He'd been there for her from the instant he'd found her on the beach.

She wanted to be there for him, too, for some reason. She was drawn to him, and she had been from the first time she'd met his beautiful dark eyes.

The feel of his warm, smooth *bare* skin against her naked body danced into her mind, and a shiver shot down Lexi's spine. It'd been brief, but she'd loved how they'd touched. She'd never felt such…intrigue and desire in her life. She wanted to explore that. She wanted more. The brush of his mouth over hers during that very brief kiss made the shiver travel to her limbs. Lexi wanted more of that, too.

A part of her wanted to tell him she wasn't from his time, but the rational part reared up again, reminding her Graeme would think her mad, or just not believe her.

"Listen, it'll take about an hour to get to my place in Calligarry, okay?" he said.

She thrummed with awareness, and wanted to be closer to him. Touching him.

What an odd driving force. Something she'd never experienced before.

Lexi had never heard of Calligarry, but she'd been

to Armadale—to the MacDonald castle—many times. That journey had taken longer than an hour from Dunvegan, but his conveyance had already shown it moved much faster than even her father's favorite stallion.

She was part-impressed and part-scared, although that was silly. She'd been in the truck several times that day, and it'd been perfectly safe.

Graeme spoke about food, and her stomach growled, as if responding aloud for her.

Their gazes brushed, and he quirked a smile. "I guess that sounds good to you, huh?"

She nodded, flashing a shy smile.

"I'm sorry for not asking you about food before now. It was rude of me."

"Nay," she said quickly. "Ye've been nothin' but kind ta me all day. I am grateful."

The smile he wore now was soft, and it did something funny to her insides.

Lexi looked down again, rubbing her hands along the trews she'd been told were called jeans. They weren't soft, but not exactly firm either. She liked how the fabric felt under her fingertips.

They were like the trews Graeme wore, but hers were darker. She liked that they were dressed similarly, too. It made her feel somehow closer to him.

He'd put his gray leine back on, stating he was too warm in the longs-sleeved one he'd worn since giving her his T-shirt, he'd called it. Unfortunately, she'd missed a peek at his bare chest when he'd changed.

Lexi's T-shirt from Flora's store was a soft pink hue

she'd always been fond of, and it fit her tightly, like the snug bodice of a gown her father had denied her permission to wear. It was too low cut, in his opinion, but she'd loved it.

She smiled, because she liked how the fabric felt against her skin, although the bra was an odd sensation. Flora had said she needed it, but she preferred nothing constricting her breasts. She would take it off the first chance she came upon. Despite the taut hold of a corset, she preferred one to the floating stiffness of the bra.

"My mother is always having a go a' me, so I know what that's like," Lexi blurted.

Graeme threw her a look. "Your mother again, huh? Do you remember something?"

She swallowed.

Why had she said that?

She'd wanted to make him feel better about his grandfather, but she needed to be careful.

Lexi had already slipped up once in Flora's shop. She needed to stop mentioning, well, anything that would could lead anyone to know she wasn't from his time.

"I...remember her, I think..."

He held her gaze for a few tense seconds, before looking back at the road. "Do you remember her name?"

Lexi's heart thumped at the dishonesty about to breech her mouth. "Nay. I remember...we had a row."

He flexed his hands on the wheel that seemed to control the truck. The apple of his throat bobbed. "Do you know what about?"

She shook her head, and her cheeks alit with fires of

lies. She glanced out the side window so she could avoid his caring eyes.

"Okay, no biggie. It'll all come back in its own time, like Doc Guinn said."

Lexi forced her stare to remain on the hilly terrain.

"Hey, like I told you on the beach, it'll be okay." Graeme reached over the bags and touched her shoulder.

She lifted her hand, and he took it, entwining their fingers.

The gesture comforted her. Filling her with a warmth she craved. The rightness of his touch was also startling but felt unmistakable at the same time.

Like it'd always been.

She tingled all over, like before when she'd thought about his body on hers, and his mouth touching her lips. "Aye," she whispered, because his silence seemed to require an answer.

They didn't talk more as the truck continued down the road that cut through lands that looked a little familiar.

Graeme held Lexi's hand for a long time.

They were getting closer to where people lived, because there were a few crofter's cabins strewn about here and there, then some closer together, as if they drew closer to a village.

"It's not much, but it's mine for the foreseeable future."

He parked the truck in the front of a modest, white cottage with a dark roof and two windows facing them. The front door was red, and there was a small step of stone in front of it. The roof was dark brown and made of an odd material. It wasn't made of thatch, like she was used to seeing.

It was much smaller than Dunvegan, but Lexi had visited similar homes when she'd accompanied her brother and MacLeod men-at-arms, collecting the rents a few times. It wasn't something common for women, let alone the laird's daughter, but she'd insisted.

To her mother's chagrin, of course.

"It's bonnie," she said, flashing a smile for Graeme.

"Not as bonnie as you," he said

Their eyes locked.

Her heart stuttered and she wanted to slide closer, to stare into his orbs of midnight even more and taste his mouth again. Share a real kiss, instead of the innocent gesture he'd given her earlier.

The idea startled and her cheeks seared for the thousandth time since she'd met this appealing MacDonald man.

Graeme averted his gaze first. "Uh, sorry. I…Not sure why I said that." He shook his head.

Lexi sucked in a breath to tamp down something that overcame her swiftly, achingly, that felt something suspiciously like hurt. "I dinnae mind," she whispered.

He laughed, and the corner of his mouth quirked up. "I'm glad to hear it, but I don't want to be an ogre. You're going through a lot, and you don't need me taking advantage of you."

She gave a sharp headshake. "Ye dinnae. I dinnae believe ye capable."

He sucked in an audible breath and held her hand to his chest.

The feel of his heart thundering under her fingertips was so tempting. Again, she wanted to move closer.

"Well, thank you for putting your trust in me. I'll help you any way I can. You'll get your memory back and we'll get you home. Your people have to know you're gone by now, and are probably worried about you. Skye isn't that big. They'll be looking for you. Mark my words."

Guilt assaulted Lexi and tears stung her eyes. She looked down, because she didn't want Graeme to sense the emotional havoc his words had just caused.

Jesu, as her Uncle Duncan would say.

Her family *was* probably worried.

She was *lying* to this kind man who'd done nothing but protect and care for her all day.

He didn't know her, and she didn't deserve Graeme MacDonald's attention.

You could fix it all by going home.

Lexi cursed the voice in the back of her head. She could. She could *blink* back to the beach, find the cave of the Faery Stones, open them and go back to 1694, where—when—she belonged.

She'd leave Graeme, to never look back.

Dread encased her heart, causing it to slowly slid toward her stomach.

She couldn't do that.

She didn't *want* to.

Did she?

"Lexi? Are you okay?" Graeme was standing to her right, inside the open truck door.

She hadn't been aware he'd gotten out, or that he'd

opened her side.

Lexi forced a nod and accepted his extended hand to help her dismount the high conveyance's cushion. Not that she needed the help, but she wanted his touch again.

When her rescuer's fingers enclosed hers and his thumb started rubbing gently back and forth, a shiver of anticipation shot down her spine. Her new clothes suddenly felt too hot and too tight.

She exhaled and met the concern in those deep dark eyes. "I—I mean, aye, I'm okay." She echoed his word choice.

The worry didn't leave Graeme's eyes.

He cleared his throat. "Well, let me show you around." He smiled, and he cocked his head toward the small home to illustrate his point.

Lexi followed him to the door.

He rifled through his pocket and pulled out a ring of what she assumed were keys from the jangling sound.

Lexi had seen keys, of course. Her Aunt Claire had a huge ring of them for all the locked doors of the castle she'd grown up in, but these keys were much smaller. She tried not to stare. She wanted to touch them, see if they were as heavy as the ones she remembered, but didn't want to ask.

The door creaked as Graeme pushed it open. He grunted. "It sticks. I keep meaning to look at it," he said. "It's not much, but I actually like it."

Lexi stepped into the dim cottage.

He moved to the right and touched the wall.

The room lit up, like...well, magic. She gasped.

"What's wrong?" His concern was back.

"No-nothin'" she pushed out, scanning the room for candles — or any other obvious signs of how he'd made the cottage come alight.

"Lexi?" Graeme asked.

She hadn't moved from the doorway.

He darted around her and pulled the red panel shut. It connected with a *thud*.

Their eyes met, and he patted his thigh with a nervous edge she could feel.

"Well, this is home," he said, gesturing around the room.

Lexi told herself to let go of the light-up spell for now, and look where he indicated. The space was a sitting room of sorts, with couches on both sides and a sizable hearth to the right. The seating was large, padded and looked inviting.

One was a dark green and ivory tartan, and the other was a solid gray that seemed to complement the green. There was also a fluffy, oversized chair of a deep red color next to the fireplace. The spot looked the coziest of all the corner.

The room was cozy, and all the mismatched pieces seemed to fit.

The dark wood floor planks went nicely with the lighter bricks of the hearth and mantel, as did the multicolored tartan rug in the center of the room.

She was in love with the place in seconds. It reminded her of her favorite sitting room in Dunvegan, but without all the windows. The ladies' solar, where her mother and aunts spent a lot of time.

The thought of home caused a new guilty ache in

her gut, but Lexi let her feet take her further into the room, and she ran her hands across the back of the green and white tartan couch. A fluffy-looking pillow sat in one corner. Under her fingers, it felt like a sheep's coat ready for shearing. She smiled.

"Like that, do you?" Graeme asked, a smile in his voice.

She nodded and threw a glance over her shoulder. "Verra much."

"Are you hungry?" He gestured to a doorway on the far left of the room she hadn't noticed. "Kitchen's that way."

"Aye."

"I'm not much of a chef, but let's see what I can come up with."

chapter eight

Graeme sighed and rolled over. His bed was comfortable and familiar, but sleep so wasn't happening.

Her first night at his place.

Lexi was in the tiny guest room across the hall from his, and she was too close. Simultaneously, she was too far away.

It made *zero* sense, but he wanted her in his bed, in his arms.

Since he'd taken her shopping for clothing and showed her around his small home, she'd opened up, like a blooming rose.

Hesitant at first, but she spoken without him talking first, and she'd explored the cottage touching everything, as if putting her mark on it.

From the moment she'd stepped inside, he'd felt like Lexi belonged there. Which made even less sense than him wanting her in his bed.

He'd warmed up some beef stew Bridget had made for him and Gramps the other day, and Lexi had devoured it, as if she hadn't eaten in days. Who the hell knew how long she'd been on the beach, so maybe it *had* been days.

She'd stared at the microwave as if it were a

mysterious contraption she'd never seen before. Nor did she know how to open the fridge.

His little foundling was more intriguing by the moment. Could amnesia make someone forget simple things like that?

Lexi had jumped when Graeme had turned on the living room lights, as if she hadn't expected it.

What was going on?

Instinct was screaming she wasn't being completely honest with him. A few times she'd mentioned her mother, but refused to answer further when pressed. What was that about? Memories returned or things that weren't quite true?

When Dr. Guinn had asked mundane childhood questions, she'd known the answers, but she didn't remember her mother's name?

Graeme hated that his suspicions gained probability that she was, in fact, lying.

Why?

What did she have to gain from lying?

It was obvious by the way he'd found her that something bad had happened to her.

As the evening had progressed, he'd felt more and more there was an iceberg of a story, even if he couldn't put his finger on the whys, whats and hows.

Damn, it'd been hard to show her to that guest room. He'd wanted to sweep her up, plant her on his bed and…

His cock twitched. He cursed. Graeme propped himself on his elbow, punched his pillow and flipped it over to the cold side. He settled back down, grumbling to himself to get it together.

The guest room wasn't much smaller than his bedroom, but it definitely had a more feminine touch. The curtains and bedding were made up of a pale green and purple plaid, and thistles embroidered on the sheets.

He'd helped her fold and place her new clothing in the sizable trunk at the end of the bed.

Somehow that had made the room feel like hers, and his gut had ached because again, he wanted her with him. In his room.

In his bed.

Graeme had never been drawn to a woman like he was to Lexi.

She's barely a woman.

She wasn't, though. Was she?

Lexi was sweet, smart and seemed more mature than twenty-one.

"Graeme?"

His name spoken in the sweet Highland brogue made his gaze shoot to the doorway. Her voice vibrated down his body, landing on the tip of his dick.

It was already interested, and jumped against the fabric containing it.

He swallowed and sat up, sending a fervent order for his little friend not to stand up, too.

Lexi stood in the entryway of his bedroom.

He hadn't even heard her open the door.

The nightlight in the hallway so he wouldn't die on the way to the bathroom—which was on the other side of the ancient cottage—silhouetted her slender profile.

She wore an old white tee of his. The damn thing

might as well have been see-through. The V-neck hung from one of her shoulders, and the curve of her hip shadowed by material was easily revealed hung to her mid-thigh.

Graeme swallowed. Hard.

Hadn't Flora given her some pajamas?

Should he curse the older woman or praise her?

Lexi was more appealing than when she'd been naked on the beach.

All his blood slowly slid south. His normally comfortable basketball shorts were suddenly too-tight. He swallowed again. "Lexi? Is something wrong?" he wanted to go to her, but he couldn't get up. Needed to get a freaking-hold of himself.

She took two steps into his room and his other motion-detected nightlight, plugged in low on the wall next to his small chest of drawers, came to life. Lexi jumped, shot it a look, then glanced back at him. She bit her plump bottom lip.

Graeme sucked back a groan and shoved his hand through his hair. "What's wrong darlin'?" His words came out as rough as he felt, so he cleared his throat.

"I...dinnae want ta be alone."

Kill me now.

"You can't sleep?" he croaked, because a distraction was needed. *Stat.* He didn't want to acknowledge what she'd just admitted, because he very much needed some self-control. His had packed bags and hopped on a plane back to Texas.

She shook her head, looking adorable and innocent with a little vixen mixed in, since her bottom lip was shiny and inviting from the treatment she'd given it.

"Do you want to get in bed with me?"

What the fuck had just come out of his mouth?

Even her small nod was a contradiction—
confidence and shyness as she inched forward, the
nightlight illuminating the short distance.

She was going to kill him, and had no idea she was
even doing it.

Graeme threw the covers back in invitation, and
Lexi paused.

Maybe sense had dawned on one of them?

He glanced down at himself. He didn't have a shirt
on, but his stiffy wasn't showing—thank God. "I won't
hurt you," he whispered. He wanted to extend a hand,
but touching her right now was the worst idea in the
universe.

Her gaze brushed his and her violet eyes seemed to
glow in the dimness of his bedroom.

"I ken that." Her words were confident and she
came to him quicker.

At least she knew he wasn't an axe murder, but did
she know how much he wanted her and how hard it
would be not to act on that?

He couldn't even kiss her.

He could *not* kiss her.

Kisses would lead to more.

More was forbidden.

Graeme had to suck back an honest-to-God gulp—
not the first time that day.

Lexi's slender knee hit the sheet and she leaned her
body forward to get onto the mattress, crawling, like the

first time she'd tried to get in the pickup. The oversized shirt also shifted, sliding down her shoulder even more, and the collar hanging low, swaying as she moved toward him. Giving Graeme an eyeful of her bare breasts.

He swallowed.

Again.

I am abso-fucking-lutely dead.

He forced himself to think of something else, something to tamp down the insane urge to pull her toward him. A prickly sahuaro cactus...a drizzly autumn day...a frigid Scottish winter. No, something even more unappealing like soggy bread pudding.

She came right to him when she was fully prone, as if she'd done so a million times.

Their bodies were so close, but not touching—like *he* wanted them to be anyway.

Graeme lay down, rolling to his side so they faced each other.

Lexi offered a shy smile and it took everything in him not to reach out and brush his fingers across her cheek.

"Is this okay?" he asked.

She nodded and shifted closer. Licked her lips, as if she was nervous. "Will...will ye hold me?"

Fuck. Me.

Lexi couldn't help but snuggle into Graeme's warmth even more. He had no shirt on, and she wanted to be even closer to his body.

When she'd seen his bare torso from the end of his bed, warning whistles had echoed in the back of her mind. She'd recalled how his bare skin had felt against hers on the beach and she'd wanted more.

No more hesitation had remained.

She wanted to be close to him like that again.

If her father knew she was in a half-naked man's bedroom, let alone joining him in his bed—well, the Laird of Clan MacLeod would've buried his claymore into Graeme's belly.

She shoved the idea away, and pushed her arm across Graeme's defined abdominal muscles, settling against his trim waist and sighing as a sense of peace settled over her.

Why had she asked him to hold her?

She'd been lying in the borrowed bed, and it was nice. Warm and more comfortable than any bed she'd ever slept in. She'd like the embroidered thistles on the linens, and had traced each one with her fingertip.

The green and purple plaid comforter was thick and inviting, but when she'd closed her eyes, all Lexi could see was home and her own room, and her parents. Her brother, and even her cousins.

Then the fight with her mother and her brother's urgings when she'd been in the cave. She wasn't where or when she belonged.

The guilt had been too much. She'd chided herself to go back to the Faery Stones and go home.

The counter-argument, of course, was if she just disappeared, now Graeme would worry that something had happened to her.

Then she'd obsessed about being close to him, and she couldn't abide being alone any longer. She'd come to his room and muttered the truth—she didn't want to be alone.

The man she'd met only that morning would make her feel better, even if Lexi couldn't offer him what she should—an honest explanation. A confession that she hadn't lost her memory.

She sucked in a breath and told herself to remain in the moment. She was with Graeme. In his bed. Like her clan's motto, she would hold fast to him.

Even as she melted into him, he seemed to stiffen. Lexi paused, lifting her head to meet his eyes. "Are ye well?"

He nodded, but his expression was stamped with discomfort. His jaw was tight, as if gritting his teeth.

"Did I hurt ye?" She started to pull away, but he grabbed her wrist and held her palm to his chest, like he had in the truck.

This time, his heated bare flesh kissed her skin, and Lexi shivered, but not because she was cold. Her tummy swirled with an unfamiliar fire.

"No, Lexi, you didn't hurt me." Graeme laughed, but it wasn't a sound full of any humor. It was dark somehow, but it didn't frighten her. "This is just crazy."

"What is?" she whispered.

"I don't want to tell you, because it will only scare you."

"Nay, I dinnae think so."

"You don't think what?"

"Ye dinnae scare me."

"If I tell you I want you more than I've ever wanted a woman in my life, it wouldn't scare you?" He laughed again, a dark sound just like before. "You don't know me. I don't know you. I found you on the beach *this morning*, but I'm drawn to you in a way I can't explain. It feels…right. You here tonight; it feels right."

Tremors chased each other down her spine, and Lexi's heart jumped to her throat. Words tumbled out. "I feel the same."

That was a truth she could offer him.

Their eyes met in the darkness of the room, and neither of them spoke.

Graeme's mouth descended, covering hers, engulfing her lips, but it felt more like her whole body.

His tongue pushed inside her with an urgent edge, rubbing against hers, encouraging it to move, dance, to play with his.

Lexi opened for him even more, and rested her hands on his muscled pectoral muscles.

He shifted his weight, pushing her flat into his bed, running his hands down her shoulders and sides, then over her bottom, caressing the curve and continuing downward to the back of her thighs.

Graeme urged her legs open and settled between them in one swift move, but he never stopped kissing her.

She kissed him back, her blood well on its way to a rolling boil. Sensations darted all over her form. Lexi had combusted from the inside out, and his weight on top of her caused an odd sense of worry and want, all wrapped together.

She'd never been touched like this.

His lips caressed her chin and nipped her neck. The roughness of unshaven cheeks made her want more, notching her need higher.

Lexi threw her head back and slipped her arms around his neck, a moan breaking free. She held on for dear life as he started to rock against her, and entwined her legs with his.

She could feel his hard length at the apex of her thighs. It was contained by his black short pants, and it should've given her pause, because she wore nothing under the oversized white leine, but all she could do was *feel*.

All she wanted to do was feel.

All she wanted was *more*.

Then his hand was there, between her legs, touching her most intimate place.

Lexi froze in his arms, gasping.

Graeme stilled, too, and their eyes met. "Lexi?" he panted.

Her cheeks seared, not from the pleasure he'd been giving her, because the change in his expression told her he *knew*.

He knew she'd never been touched.

Never been kissed.

Graeme knew she was innocent.

"Lexi?" he repeated.

She swallowed.

He pulled his body off her, sitting upright next to her.

Lexi missed his heat immediately, and wanted to rush back into his arms, feel his body against hers. She scrambled to a sitting position next to him, looking away and was grateful her hair curtained her face. Couldn't look him in the eye.

"Hey," he whispered, cupping her cheeks and making her meet his gaze. "Talk to me."

She shook her head, but couldn't bring herself to break away from his touch. "In the truck, when ye kissed me...'twas my first."

Graeme was quiet for two heartbeats, then four. The apple of his throat bobbed and he made a sound he quickly cut off. "Ever?"

Lexi hollered at herself to be brave. "Aye."

"Jesus Christ," he spat.

She flinched and reared back.

"No, no, that was for me, not you. I'm so sorry!" He tugged her closer, and she didn't fight him.

She settled in his arms, wrapping hers around his middle. Lexi let Graeme hold her, because it was what she wanted anyway.

"I'm sorry," he said again, running his hands over her hair and down her back, making large circles over the white leine she'd nicked from his room. "I'm a freaking overbearing asshole, and I never should have told you I wanted you. I never should've kissed you like that. I'm so sorry."

He said a few curses under his breath she'd heard her Aunt Claire say before and, in a way, it made her want to smile.

She gathered her courage around her like a cape,

and pushed back from him gently. Lexi reached for his stubbled cheek and Graeme stilled, but he didn't shove her away.

He caressed her arm, elbow and the back of her hand, then held her fingers to his face.

"Dinnae apologize," she said. "I dinnae regret...anathin.'"

"What?" His beautiful dark eyes went wide.

"When ye kissed me this mornin', I wanted more. I wanted what happened here, in yer bed. What ye tol' me, 'bout wantin' me...I want ye, too."

Graeme's mouth fell open and a strangled sound came out. He cleared his throat and tried again. "Are you a virgin?" he blurted.

Lexi nodded, because she couldn't form the words.

"Then I have no business kissing you. Or touching you there." He shook his head.

Hurt washed over her, and she had to move away from him. Her eyes smarted but she refused to cry.

She regretted nothing.

It didn't matter that he'd been right.

They *didn't* know each other. They *had* met just that morning.

None of it mattered. The draw he'd mentioned was something she felt, too.

Strongly...like magic. The same magic that lived deep in her bones and sung at her fingertips when she called upon it.

Lexi wanted more; she'd just been startled when his hand had explored where only her own fingers had ever been before.

She ached there even now, from want.

Want for Graeme MacDonald.

Her mother and her aunts had explained what happened between a man and woman. Just because she was innocent didn't mean she was naïve.

She just hadn't expected to be so…overwhelmed by him.

"Hey, hey…" Graeme said, urging her back to him, and tilting her chin up. "This is on me, not you. I shouldn't have…"

Anger shot up from her gut and Lexi grabbed his face with both hands. She slammed her lips into his and kissed the breath out of him, which whooshed against her mouth.

She forced her tongue into his mouth, but it only took Graeme seconds to kiss her back.

They fought each other for control, but at least he wasn't denying her anymore.

Lexi kissed him with all the desperation she felt, even if she couldn't understand why she was feeling so much for him, so fast.

It might not make sense, as he'd mentioned, but it was true that she felt right in his arms, with his mouth moving over hers like this.

"Lexi, stop," he murmured against her lips.

Again, hurt assaulted when Graeme backed away from their kiss.

"I'm gonna come in my shorts." He panted through the words, but when their gazes brushed, he was smirking. His enticing mouth was swollen from hers.

"Dinnae deny me," she breathed, but it was still a

demand.

He stilled. "I hurt you. I hurt your feelings." It wasn't a question. Graeme sighed and shoved his hands through his sandy brown locks, like he'd done when she'd come into his bedroom. "I can't do anything fucking right."

It was Lexi's turn to smirk. That wasn't true. One touch or kiss from him set her on fire.

That was right.

"Can I start over?" he whispered.

"Aye."

"I'm not rejecting you, Lexi. It's just...I'm thirty. You're twenty-one..."

"So?" Lexi asked, cocking her head to one side. Her mother was years older than her father, but she was Fae, so she didn't look it. Not like she could tell that to Graeme MacDonald.

She'd known men older than Graeme take wives younger than she.

"You're a virgin. That's not for me."

It stung, but she could tell he was explaining, not trying to hurt her. "'Tis *my* innocence." Annoyance chased some of the pain away.

He was being like her mother, telling her what to do. Wasn't he?

She'd just found him, discovered what desire felt, been teased with first licks of pleasure.

Lexi had been honest when she'd admitted wanting him. She was curious. She liked him. It was also true that she did feel genuine rightness when she was close to him.

He made her feel safe.

Graeme paused, as if trying to gauge what she was trying to say. "Exactly."

"'Tis mine," she reiterated. "Mine ta do with what I wish."

He didn't speak right away, and he averted his eyes before meeting her gaze again. "It's not my place."

"Ye dinnae want me?"

Graeme groaned. "Don't do this to me."

"Say it," she ordered.

"Just because I want you doesn't mean it's *right*."

Lexi grabbed his hand and cupped it to her breast. Her nipple tingled at the contact, through the thin fabric of the white leine.

He made a pained noise in his throat.

"Ye...ye make me *feel*..." She closed her eyes and smiled when he pushed a soft kiss into the tender flesh of her throat.

"You make me feel, too. That's probably part of the problem," he groused.

"I want ta feel...more."

Graeme threw her a serious look. "I'm not taking your virginity tonight."

Lexi smiled in triumph and kissed him.

He'd said *tonight*.

Not, *not at all*.

chapter nine

"Alana, wait!"

Alana stormed down the beach, ignoring her sister-by-marriage. She lifted the skirts she'd just donned. Trews would've helped her navigate the loamy ground faster. That was the same as in the past, evidently. However, her favorite pair, made of a fine material in her realm of birth and in her favorite hue of dark purple, were missing. Likely lost. Another thing to add to the discourse she needed to have with her daughter. She'd had them since she was a lass herself, and she was fond of them.

Traveling through time, using the Faery Stones had stripped their clothing, but a magic sack had let them bring garments.

She, her son's wife, and Claire had gotten dressed in the dimness of the cave.

"We can't just run off. You've never been to this time! Slow down." Duncan's wife huffed, as she caught up, Alana's daughter-by-marriage in tow.

Lila was unusually silent, but didn't fail to keep up.

Alana kept moving, not giving into the wince when a sharp stone bit into her heel through her thin slippers. She should've worn boots.

Her two companions exchanged low words, but she didn't wait for them.

It'd taken everything in her soul not to use magic on their husbands to get them to stay in 1694. Claire — and her sister Jules — had helped convince their highlanders there was no danger by to coming to Claire's and Lila's time without them. Duncan and Alex couldn't rush into what was called "modern days" with claymores drawn.

Her son, Angus, had been more reasonable. He'd actually listened to his wife.

Lila had had the most recent experience with the century she'd traveled from, after all.

"Seriously! Dressed like this, we're going to stick out. People will think you're from some Renaissance Faire, despite us still being in Scotland."

Alana was familiar with the term, because of stories Claire had told many times, but she didn't pause. She couldn't. "My daughter has been gone for days. I shall not wait any longer."

Again, Lila spoke, but like before, it was to Claire, not Alana.

Her sister-by-marriage threw her hands in the air, then physically impeded her path, and her son's wife came to stand beside her, forming a female wall.

Pretty blonde Claire was only a little taller, and her long blonde hair was pulled back in a thick plait, not a gray in sight. Despite birthing three sons, she was slender, and looked younger than her nearly fifty years. "Alana. Think for a minute, okay?" She was dressed in a simple green shift, which was her favorite color and brought out the color of her eyes.

She sighed. Didn't want to meet her gaze. She didn't want to look at either woman right now.

Lila was also dressed in a simple shift dress, but a soft blue color.

"Mother—" she started.

It'd always made Alana happy that the surgeon from the future wanted to refer to her as such, but at the moment, it only irritated. "Nay," she barked.

"We will find her. It will be all right." Claire lowered her voice and touched Alana's wrist, so she would finally look at her.

"Please, just listen to us, before you go storming around," Lila said. She scanned the area, assessing with her physician's eye, as she often did. Her long dark hair hung loose to her hips, and swayed in the breeze. "How are we going to find her, anyway?"

"Here." Alana tapped her forehead, then her chest over her heart. "I know where she is already. I can sense her. I only have to follow what I feel."

"Oh, great," Claire breathed, but sounded more like than exasperation than relief.

Alana arched an eyebrow. "What?"

"You can't just run off." Her sister-by-marriage repeated Lila's earlier sentiment, but this time Claire didn't sound so frantic. "This may be Skye, but it's not like you know it."

"It matters not." Alana held her head high, like the princess she'd been born to be.

"Alana."

Her name held warning.

"Mother," Lila echoed.

The two women remained shoulder-to-shoulder, blocking her path.

Reminiscent of her husband, Alana growled from her throat.

Claire arched a fair eyebrow.

"I have come here to get my daughter, and I shall."

"Oh, no," her sister-by-marriage said, but she glanced at the youngest woman of their party, and her mouth rippled as if she was fighting a smile.

"What?" Alana demanded.

"She's being all regal, like the Fae Queen of Scotland."

Lila made an amused snort, as if stifling a laugh.

Alana frowned. Her husband always accused her of acting queenly when she didn't want to be argued with, and she'd never admitted so.

Wasn't about to this day, either.

She didn't have time to rise to Claire's tease, she needed to find Alexandria.

The feeling of her daughter's location in her mind was faint—the lass wasn't close. Yet, she couldn't be overly far, either, or Alana wouldn't have been able to sense her at all.

Alarm washed over her. Did the faintness of the signal mean something was wrong with Alexandria? Was she hurt?

Or worse.

Alana sucked in a breath and shoved the thought away.

Nay, it couldn't be so.

She concentrated and tried to gather her powers inward.

Tapping into her magic was even more difficult than the century she belonged in. It was...sluggish to respond, as if it, too, had been left in the past.

The Human Realm had always made magic a challenge, but Alana hadn't expected *this*.

Her tummy jumped.

Doubt edged the corners of her mind.

What if she couldn't find her daughter?

She forced another breath and looked into Claire's green eyes, before meeting the dark brown ones of her daughter-by-marriage. She closed her own for two heartbeats and braced herself. "What do you suggest we do?"

Claire and Lila exchanged a glance.

Graeme didn't say much on the drive back to his cottage, but he'd white-knuckled the wheel that controlled the truck's direction the truck.

They'd left Dunvegan for the evening, and twilight had just crested the horizon. Streaks of pink and orange stretched across the sky, and a touch of fiery yellow smudged the line where the sun went to bed for the night.

Lexi hadn't made out the words of the row Graeme had with his grandfather. Yet, the raised voices and clattering noises were loud enough to wake the dead, well-heard from the other room she was in. Her rescuer-turned-lover had stalked to the blue truck, his shoulders vibrating with frustration. She felt the tension rolling off him even now.

"Graeme?" she ventured.

He stilled, then threw her a smile that came off as insincere.

She frowned.

She wanted to reach for him, soothe those worry lines off his forehead, but kept her hands in her lap, resisting the urge.

The man brooded so hard.

"Are ye well?" Lexi murmured.

Graeme sighed and his chest heaved with a breath. "I will be, thanks." This time, the curve of his lips turned gentle and sweet.

"Okay," she said, using his word. "If ye wanna talk, I wanna listen." Lexi borrowed the words from her Aunt Claire.

She could feel Graeme's pain after the negative interaction with his grandfather, and it made her heart ache—and think about her mother. More specifically, how angry she always was after a lecture or argument.

His laugh was low, but not unpleasant. "I appreciate that, I really do. But you already have a lot going on. No sense in piling more on you."

"'Tis nay a bother. Yer so kind ta me. I wanna be tha' fer ye."

Graeme reached for her hand, squeezed, then brought her knuckles to his lips. He pressed a warm kiss there.

A tremor raced up her wrist and into her forearm, making her heart skip, and her cheeks sear. Desire tickled beneath the surface of her skin, and her belly quivered.

The rest of the ride was almost too quiet, but she felt less of the strain that'd seized his wide shoulders. He still held her hand in his much larger one.

Soon, they pulled in front of the cottage, and Lexi was eager to go inside, into his bedroom and taste him again, like she had last night.

Perhaps go further.

Graeme opened the red door, and it squeaked the same protest it had the night before. He gestured for her to enter the cottage, then hung his keys on the hook and closed things up.

Lexi grabbed his hand.

"Lexi?" he whispered, but didn't pull away.

She licked her lips, and his dark gaze glued to her mouth.

A hunger rose in his eyes, one like a hungry wolf staring at his prey, starving for a meal.

It spurred her on.

"I wanna make ye feel better."

The barest hint of a smile played at the corners of his mouth. "Yeah?"

She slid forward, slipping her arms around his neck and pressing her lips to his.

Graeme didn't hesitate to kiss her back. He rubbed his tongue against hers.

Lexi shuddered into his muscled chest, pressing closer, until he wrapped her in his arms.

"Take me ta yer bed," she breathed into his mouth.

"Aren't...you...hungry?" he panted, leaning back to meet her eyes.

"Aye. Fer yer body on mine." She didn't question where the courage had come from. Lexi recalled his touch from the night before and just wanted more. He could call her wanton, and she would own it. Beg him to take her.

He groaned, and kissed her again, this time harder, and it left her head spinning in a hazy desire for him. For more.

Getting to his room and undressed was a blur.

She lay naked in his bed, waiting for him, eager and burning from the inside out for his touch. For his mouth on her.

Graeme shucked his shirt and jeans, but when he joined her in his bed, he still wore his gray short pants.

Lexi frowned, and their gazes brushed.

"It doesn't need to be too much too fast," he said.

"I want ye."

The smile he flashed was tender. "I want you, too. But—"

She tugged him down, wrapping her arms around his neck again and kissing his protest away. Lexi moaned when his chest brushed her breasts, his chest hair teasing, shooting tingles down her limbs.

Graeme didn't pull away.

He kissed her expertly, winding his tongue around hers, exploring her mouth as she explored his in return. He let her hold him even tighter, and his hands started to roam her body, teasing her nipples into hard peaks and making her blood boil.

Lexi got lost in the sensations, breaking away from his mouth only when she needed a breath, and tossing her head back on the pillows that smelled like him.

"Lexi."

Her name was strained, and made her look into his face.

He was gorgeous, his cheeks flushed, and sandy locks mussed. His lips looked well-used and his chest heaved as he struggled for control and breathing alike.

It made her want him even more.

"Have you ever had an orgasm?" Graeme caressed her inner thigh, his fingertips moving ever closer to her most private place.

"Or...or...gasm?" she whispered, struggling to concentrate when she throbbed where he wasn't touching her yet. Where she needed him to touch her.

Lexi had frozen at the first brush of his hand last night. She wouldn't tonight.

She wanted his hand there, to see how it felt.

"Have you ever touched yourself until you climaxed?"

Her cheeks burned, but not from arousal. She'd heard of women touching themselves, but she had never done so, other than cleaning herself in the bath.

Should she admit that to her lover?

Lexi shook her head. "I've ne'er..." She couldn't make the rest of the words form, so she averted her gaze.

"You've never pleasured yourself?" His question was low, curious.

"'Tis...'tis nay proper," she finally pushed out.

Graeme's chuckle was warm. "Of course, it isn't. Neither is this. But..."

"But?" Lexi met his pretty dark eyes and smiled at his amusement.

Her mirth quickly faded, replaced with anticipation because of the intensity in his handsome face. Something that felt akin to magic shot all over her body.

"Let me show you." The apple of his throat bobbed, as if he needed to fortify himself.

"Aye. Show me pleasure."

He groaned and kissed her again, his hands moving in tandem with his mouth and tongue. Graeme cupped her breasts, then her sides and stomach. He burned a trail of warm wet kisses down her neck and across her collarbone.

Lexi whimpered and writhed, then gasped when he sucked one of her nipples in his mouth. She buried her hands in his hair, compelled to hold onto something solid.

He licked and sucked his way down her belly, until she could remain still no longer.

She had to pant to get air down, and her whole form warmed, searing inside and out.

"More?" Graeme asked, pressing a kiss below her navel.

She moaned.

His laugh vibrated against her lower belly. "I'll take that as a yes." He didn't pause for Lexi to speak again— but it wasn't likely she could.

Graeme gently pushed her legs wider and settled between them. He pressed his thumb into the tight bundle of nerves at the top of her sex.

Sensation shot upward, and she screamed.

Then his mouth was there, where his fingers had been, and he circled the nub with his tongue. He probed below at the same time, gently sliding a finger into her.

Coherent thought fled. Ecstasy made her shake from head to toe.

"Damn, you're tight and so wet already."

Lexi squirmed and wiggled, until he grabbed her hips gently to hold her in place.

"Just feel, Lexi. Let go, and let me make you feel good."

She forced a nod, and forced her shoulders to relax into the bed.

Graeme licked her sex and she called his name, her hips shooting up of their own accord.

He chuckled. "You're so hot, darlin'. You taste fantastic."

She couldn't form words to answer him. Lexi threw her head back again.

He kept mapping her sex with his tongue, and thrusting one finger in, then two, and moving in and out of her in a rhythm that made her want more.

Something was building.

Something warm and pulsing inside her, throbbing as it went, gained speed and intensity, demanding more, ignited by his touches, his licks, his caresses.

She couldn't remain still, and her hips bobbed up over and over but Graeme kept squeezing her sides, holding her, as he continued his ministrations.

The feeling peaked, her heart racing feeling like she

was about to tumble, to explode, to do something she couldn't possibly explain. She had no idea what her body was going to do, but whatever it was, it was imminent.

Finally, she stiffened from head to toe. She crushed her eyes shut so hard she saw stars.

Pleasure exploded below, right where he touched and tasted her.

"That's it, Lexi-darlin'. Let go. Come for me." His words were low and steady, but also thick with desire.

He kissed her inner thigh next to her sex and caressed her there, as warmth spread through her limbs, making her feel like jam spread across freshly baked bread. Her muscles loosened eventually, so she could collapse into the bed.

She took one breath, then another, as her vision cleared and she could see again. Lexi was content all over, and her heart skipped as it also slowed, coming down from its frantic canter.

Graeme shot up her body, cradling her against him, and he pressed his lips to her forehead. His smile was soft when their gazes brushed.

"More, Graeme, I want more."

He squeezed her tighter and kissed her.

chapter ten

I love Scotland, but in the eight months I've been here, I've yet to have a decent cup of coffee, so I had my buddy ship me a ton from the US."

Lexi smiled against the warm cup he'd handed her, cradling it close to her mouth. She liked listening to him talk, so she didn't ask all the questions his words elicited. She'd heard the accent before, of course, from Aunt Claire, Aunt Jules and Lila, but when Graeme spoke, it sounded different, more appealing. She could listen to him talk for hours, no matter the subject. It was…fascinating.

She'd been with Graeme at his small cottage for three days now, and she loved every moment. She'd thought about her parents and Dunvegan often, but the guilt was fading—mostly.

Two steamy nights with her rescuer-turned-lover had certainly helped with that.

Two nights of Graeme making her *feel*. Exploring her body with his hands and tongue. Two nights of her exploring his the same.

He'd given Lexi her first orgasm, and second and third, but he hadn't taken her innocence. He introduced her to pleasure but he wouldn't complete it.

She wanted more, but he kept going on about being

too old for her, so she was determined to show him she knew her own mind.

Graeme hadn't turned her away when she'd wanted to touch and taste him. He'd shown her what he liked, and she loved being the one to have the control of making him squirm and groan, not to mention climax.

A tremor of ecstasy aftershocks made her sit taller and she forced her focus on what he was saying. This was her second morning with the dark drink, and she liked it.

She'd heard of coffee before because her Aunt Claire lamented often about not having any. It did exist in her time but it was a luxury, rather expensive and very hard to find — at least on the isle.

The coffee maker gurgled and released steam as Graeme put what he'd called a carafe back against it, and it settled in with a clicking sound.

She let her eyes wander the kitchen and all the small devices on the counter. Her gaze landed on what he'd called a microwave. Lexi still didn't understand what everything did, but the little black box heated food with the speed of magic.

A large rectangular item in the corner looked like a skinny wardrobe held food and milk — and it was cold inside, again, like magic.

It was all so fascinating, and she had a hard time not touching each and every item, running her fingers over each smooth or textured surface.

Instead of the three cooking hearths like at Dunvegan, there was a large black box-like thing built into the wall next to the microwave. The door opened outward, and Graeme had called it an oven.

There were other things in the kitchen she didn't know the name of yet, and it wasn't like she could ask. One was a flat surface with four dark circles and knobs of some sort to the side. A fancy kettle sat on one of the round spots. It was red. He hadn't used it her presence yet, so there was no telling what it did.

Lexi took it all in, cataloging everything, committing it to memory. Eventually she would know every appliance and be able to use it, no matter how much time it took. She was determined.

She stilled on the stool of the short bar and took another sip of coffee. Normally when she contemplated staying in the future for a long time — or maybe forever — guilt would bite at her.

It hadn't happened that time.

After all, she'd been intimate with a man. In her time, that meant marriage.

Lexi almost choked.

Marriage?

To Graeme?

Away from her family and everything she'd ever known for the rest of her life?

Lexi wasn't afraid of the prospect, and her heart cracked at the thought of leaving him — as much as it did when she imagined staying.

When she'd been a wee lassie, she'd fantasized about getting married in the chapel on the grounds of Dunvegan, in her best and prettiest gown. Like her parents and grandparents before her. Even her uncles and aunts — as well her brother and Lila. They'd all been wedded in that small holy place.

Could she marry without her family present?

In the wrong century?

If her father ever discovered how her MacDonald from the future had touched her, kissed her...well, the laird would kill him. Or drag them in front of a priest.

Her mother always went on and on about fate.

Was Graeme MacDonald *her* fate?

She took another sip of coffee, and closed her eyes, needing a distraction. The warm, rich flavor rolled over her tongue and she swallowed, enjoying the aftertaste filling her mouth.

Graeme's chuckle brought her back from her musing, and their gazes locked.

"You like coffee almost as much as me." He flashed a grin, which made her stomach flip.

"I've ne'er tasted the like."

His eyes danced with amusement. "You Scots and your tea."

"Aye, tea with honey. Also, mead, when my father allows it. I snuck his whisky once."

He cocked his head. "Mead? That's honeyed wine, isn't it? It sounds...old school."

Lexi's face heated. She'd slipped again. She was going to give herself away. So, she wouldn't have to answer him, she averted her gaze.

"Your father? Did you remember something?" He leaned against the basin.

She cursed herself. "Nay. I mean, I am no' certain." She couldn't look at him but she could feel his eyes on her. Lexi didn't move or look up from the mug.

"Well, we'd better get going. We need to meet Gramps at Dunvegan." Graeme turned away from her and set his mug in the washbasin.

Her pulse slowed to normal since he was appearing to drop her slip-up. She was getting use to the water coming out when he lifted the faucet's handle, but she'd gasped the first time. Then proceeded to push it up and pull it down dozens of times in fascination.

Just like when she'd realized how the living room— Graeme's word for the sitting room—had come to light up without a fire from the magical button on the wall. Lexi had turned the lights on and off again, marveling.

He'd muttered something like, "It's like she's never seen electricity before."

Her favorite was the shower. Like warm, clean rain whenever one wanted it. From the first one with Graeme—which had consisted of more kisses and touches than washing—she was addicted.

The second one she'd taken had been alone, and she'd stayed under the spray until the hot water ran out, and her new lover complained about the water bill, whatever that was.

Getting in the truck was easier, and Lexi was more comfortable now. She could put the seatbelt on and the conveyance didn't scare her, even when Graeme drove so fast the scenery of her isle was blurred.

They made it back to the castle in which she'd grown up in no time, and he'd held her hand much of the way.

She'd often seen her parents touch like that, as well as her aunts and uncles, and even her brother and his wife. It was as if being in proximity with each other wasn't enough, they had to touch in some small manner. Before Graeme, she'd never understood what had to be a compulsion to do so. Now, she did. When Graeme wasn't touching her, she craved his hands on her, anywhere.

Lexi studied his profile as he turned the truck down the path that took them around to the back of Dunvegan, where they would meet the elder MacDonald and start work for the day.

Her MacDonald had a strong jaw and straight nose, and even from the side, he was so handsome it took her breath. His hair was short, but would soon need a trim. She loved running her hands through the sandy brown locks' softness.

She loved resting her cheek against his, inhaling his clean masculine scent and closing her eyes. Whether or not he was sending her spiraling, she felt an overwhelming need to be near him.

Graeme caught her staring, and threw a smile her way as he parked next to his grandfather's other work truck, a dark green conveyance similar to theirs. It was older than this one, he'd told her.

"What is it?" he asked.

Lexi shook her head, and her cheeks heated all over again.

He laughed, and it was soft and sweet. Then he pulled her hand to his mouth and pressed a kiss to the back of her knuckles.

An accompanying shiver shot down her spine.

What was this man doing to her?

She'd known him mere days, and her heart fluttered when he looked at her. Her soul sang like the melody of the Faery Stones when he touched her.

Lexi swallowed.

She was in so much trouble.

She should go home immediately.

How could she bear to leave him now?

"Lexi? Are you okay? You look upset." Graeme paused his exit of the truck, his hand on the open door.

"I do?" Lexi met his gaze and forced a smile, then shook her head again. "I'm braw. No worries."

He grinned when she used the phrase he was fond of.

She slid to her feet and shut the truck's door, tugging the pale purple T-shirt straight. Little purple stars of a darker hue were printed across the front, and she liked it almost as much as the pink one. She'd matched it with another pair of dark blue jeans, and the trews were also a new favorite.

The white shoes Graeme had called sneakers were sturdier than the ladies' slippers she was used to, and Lexi preferred them to boots, like Graeme tended to wear. They were comfortable.

Even when she'd borrowed her cousin, Liam's, boots and used a spell to shrink them to fit her feet, they'd always end up hurting her toes after wearing them for a few hours. The white sneakers felt as if they'd been made for her.

She dashed to Graeme's side.

He ruffled in the toolbox of the bed of the truck and pulled out what he called a canvas bag of some supplies his grandfather needed. They'd picked them up at the elder MacDonald's shop the night before.

Lexi lifted it and put her arm through the straps, resting them on her shoulder.

"You don't have to get that, I will," Graeme chided.

"I'm braw," she returned quickly.

He looked her up and down. "I should stop underestimating you, Lexi MacLeod."

"Aye, ye should."

He winked, and Lexi giggled like she hadn't since she was a wee lassie.

Graeme grinned. "Let's go find the old grouch."

She frowned. "Yer grandfa may be gruff, but he cares fer ye, Graeme."

She'd watched the two men the day before. They had a hard time working together, mostly because James MacDonald didn't want to need help.

Lexi had seen how he favored his left side, and Graeme had said his grandfather had broken a hip, and subsequently had it replaced, whatever that meant. How could one have a portion of their body *replaced*?

"Could've fooled me," he muttered.

Her new lover wanted the man's approval so desperately she could feel it, despite her not being much of an empath like her mother. He wanted it so badly, it was always thick in the air when the men were together.

Instinct told Lexi that James wanted Graeme with him, but he couldn't admit it. Graeme wanted to learn more about his grandfather's trade but the two men didn't know how to communicate.

Graeme had told her his grandfather was the only

family he had remaining on his father's side.

Could she help bridge the gap between them?

Her mother's beautiful face popped into her head, and guilt assailed her. She couldn't communicate with the woman who'd given her life, either.

Lexi swallowed a sigh and held the heavy bag to her side.

"Something wrong?" Graeme asked.

"Nay." If she mentioned her mother, and how she could relate, it would make him question her even more.

"Well, Dunvegan awaits." He gestured, bowing at the waist, before hefting some sort of a tool in his strong arms.

She giggled again and followed him to the castle entrance.

chapter eleven

lana's desperation was alive, wrapping around her, constricting her like a too-tight bodice, making her heart flutter and her chest ache from mere breathing.

They hadn't found her daughter, and after searching the day before, she'd led them back to the cave of the Faery Stones where they'd bedded down for the night.

Claire had urged her to take them home, stating they could always come back, but she'd refused. Her knowledge of time travel and whether or not the passage of time was linear was unknown, so Alana couldn't risk leaving and coming back. They might not be able to return to this exact time again. She needed to get Alexandria and bring her home now.

The first day on the beach, she'd felt her daughter's magic so far away. She had to fight for balance and not even meditating made the signal clearer.

They'd trekked to Dunvegan, but her daughter wasn't there. Her eyes and her magic had told her so.

Her husband's ancestral home had been recognizable, even this far in the future. Alana marveled at the stone façade, as if recently washed by the rains, the soot and dirt cleansed from the chimneys and doorways.

Claire and Lila had tried to make their clothing a little less obvious, and they'd entered the castle with a group of people her sister-by-marriage had called tourists.

The interior of their home looked vastly different, yet still felt like home in many ways. They hadn't stayed long, when it was evident Alexandria was not present.

"Alana," Claire said her name, as if it had not been the first time. "We're out of food, let's just go home."

"Nay." She met leaf green eyes. "Let me concentrate and find her. I feel as if it will be today."

"What do you want to do, Mother?" Lila asked. "Return to Dunvegan?"

"The magic will tell me." Alana ignored the doubt in her loved ones' mirrored expressions, and sat next to the Faery Stones. Maybe sitting next to the only Fae things in this realm and century would help.

She inhaled a full calming breath and held it in until her lungs stung before releasing it. She whispered a spellword to help her slip into a trance.

Alana concentrated solely on her daughter. The child was physically gorgeous, the perfect meld of her and Alex, with her eyes and her husband's dark MacLeod hair. She was petite—also like Alana, and had a beautiful soul, despite her stubbornness. A double-dose inherited from both her parents, despite her husband's playful accusations.

Alexandria was too much like her, which was why they always clashed.

Did the lass know how much Alana loved her?

Her trance faltered as emotion rose from her gut, but she shoved it down and mentally threw the magic away from her body, sending it out to probe.

Alana reached for the nearest Faery Stone and it hummed to life, a melody reverberating outward and making her body shudder. She fed off the magic of the stone, stroking it and humming the tune.

At first the response was faint, but she felt Alexandria's magic answer back.

Would her daughter know she was probing for her?

Alana opened her eyes and found herself on her feet, with both of her hands on the glowing Faery Stone at the center of the half circle.

She hadn't recalled moving from a seated position.

Alana pushed away from the magic crystal and glanced at her family members.

Claire stared intently and expectantly, and Lila wrung her hands, her upper body pitched forward. Neither woman spoke, but their eyes shouted questions.

Alana took a deep breath and flashed a smile. "I know where she is."

The journey to the castle was a rushed jog over craggy land. Alana had been tempted to *blink*—it would've been faster, but she wouldn't have been able to travel with Claire and Lila, and neither woman would be fond of the prospect of being left behind.

Her magic was too depleted here, and even with its ordinary potency, not even in the Fae realm was she convinced she could *blink* with two other people in tow. Her cousin Xander, who was married to her husband's sister, Janet, was much stronger, and could've helped with his magic, but she'd relied on him to keep Alex and Duncan calm—and in 1694.

"Oh my God, there she is!" Claire pointed from a rocky embankment near the water toward the castle.

They approached the rear of Dunvegan's castle grounds, minus the stone wall and into what remained of the bailey from their time.

There were two modern conveyances, one blue and one green, among some others of various colors in a small *parking lot*, Claire had called it.

Alexandria stood with a man next to the blue one, but the couple was on the move within a few moments, in the opposite direction from where Alana and her companions watched.

They were still some distance away, and even if Alexandria or the man peered their way, they likely wouldn't be in view just yet. The angle was wrong and the ground not completely open. However, the couple seemed to be absorbed in their tasks—or each other.

If she could've drawn on magic, Alana would've cast an invisibility spell, but it would sap too much energy in this century and likely not be effective.

She could not tear her eyes away from the two figures dressed in attire from the current century. Clothing Claire and Lila were no doubt familiar with.

Her daughter looked...ethereal.

Alana sucked back a gasp.

Her youngest child was clad in dark trews and a fitted purple leine. She was carrying a large light-colored sack of some sort, and looking up at a tall, sandy-haired man. Her long ebony locks hung free and floated in the morning breeze, dancing over her shoulders as if they were trying to entertain.

Alexandria laughed at something the man said, and she seemed to...glow.

Her child seemed so happy, free of all burdens or sour attitudes.

Alana tripped on her next step forward, and Claire's hand landed on her forearm to steady her.

"Well, she's safe," Lila whispered. "That's good at least. The twenty-first century looks good on her, actually."

Alana tried to advance, but her sister-by-marriage squeezed harder.

"Wait," Claire said, urgency wrapped around the word. "He can't see us."

"Whyever not?" she demanded. "She is my child."

"She's a grown arse woman, Alana." Claire was probably the only one, save her husband, who would speak as such to her. The woman's time in the past had born a combined American-Scottish accent, so the sentence sounded off.

"Mother, future or past, Lexi is an adult, as much as you don't want to see it."

Alana wanted to turn and glare at her son's wife, even if she adored her. "She does no' behave so."

"I can't disagree with you there, but she saved my baby's life, so after taking time to reflect, Duncan and I

can't be as sore toward her, exposed magic or not."
Claire crossed her arms over her chest, her long blonde
plait dancing with the movement.

Alana sighed. Her daughter had been reckless, but
the youngest MacLeod, Iain, *had* been saved. If the lad
had fallen from the tree he'd had no business climbing,
he could've been seriously injured — or worse. He'd been
very high up. The only reason Iain was alive was because
of Lexi.

Alana watched her daughter disappear with the tall
man into the castle. A different entrance than the day
before with the tourists.

What were they doing?

Had Alexandria just arrived at the Dunvegan of the
far future and moved in, as if she'd never left the century
she belonged in?

"I have come for my daughter. I shall bring my
daughter home."

"Look, nothing has changed from yesterday. We
can't storm the castle, we need to get her alone," Claire
said, ever the annoying voice of reason.

As she spoke, she headed toward Dunvegan, and
soon they were standing not far from the blue and green
vehicles.

"Look at that," Lila said, her dark eyes wide.

Alana followed her daughter-by-marriage's gaze.

"Oh my," Claire whispered.

Both conveyances displayed the same marking on
the side. Alana moved closer to make out the lettering.

"MacDonald Restoration," Claire read aloud as Alana's eyes traced the words. "Lexi's got herself a MacDonald man. Jules would be so proud."

Alana pursed her lips when her sister-by-marriage laughed. She again wanted to retort that her daughter had no man, but the word stalled.

She might not have been close enough to study the sandy-haired man's face, but Alexandria had been looking up at him with affection, in the very least.

Was he the reason her daughter hadn't come home, or had something else kept her in a century she shouldn't be in?

She cleared her throat and exchanged a glance with Claire. "Alexandria will come home with us."

"What if she doesn't want to?" Lila's innocent query caused a dagger in Alana's heart.

Her daughter had reached her majority, it was true, but Alexandria wasn't ready to be on her own.

She hadn't yet been courted or married, partly because Alex would not force their daughter to marry a man she did not love, but also because Alana believed she was not ready. Too headstrong, unwilling to listen, and more reckless than she was mature.

She looked over the two women she loved dearly, who had both joined Clan MacLeod by leaving their own century and everything they'd ever known to remain at the side of a man *Alana* had always believed they'd been destined for.

Had Claire not been sucked back in time, Alana and Alex might not have gotten free of imprisonment by her own father, the Fae king, in the Fae realm.

Alex might've even died. The love of her life, her undeniable destiny.

Alexandria might never even have been born.

She sucked in a breath and swallowed.

She'd always believed in fate.

What if her daughter's was unfolding now?

Far from when she'd been born.

Away from a family that loved her.

Alana *refused* to accept that.

Alexandria wasn't ready, but she wasn't ready to let her go, either.

"It will no' come to that," she said aloud.

chapter twelve

L exi smiled when James asked Graeme to hand him a tool without barking an order as he was prone to do.

She watched the men work together in relative peace.

The elder MacDonald was restoring the double hearths of the great hall...a room that looked vastly different in her own century, without the exposed wood beams she was used to, and the white walls that made the room feel larger.

Graeme's grandfather had explained his current task was to repair and restore the mantle, hearth and fireplace to its elegant appearance dating back to the late 1700s.

It wasn't like she could mention she was familiar with how it looked about one hundred years before *that* incarnation.

As a master restoration specialist, James MacDonald had a major been part of the massive ten-year Dunvegan project as well, so he'd spent a great deal of time inside her ancestral home, and how it looked today had a great deal to do with him and his skill.

Lexi was in genuine awe of the older man and his talent to care for things otherwise long lost to the past.

Could she tell him the truth?

He'd mentioned the Fae a few times, and according to Graeme, like other Isle of Skye residents, James MacDonald believed in what he called the Faery Folk.

When he looked at her, sometimes it did seem as if he was looking *into* her, like he could see all her secrets. It was unsettling, especially since his eyes were so like Graeme's.

The thick brogue and the American affect melded together as the two MacDonald men worked and talked.

James must've been feeling generous that morning, because he was giving his grandson a gift; he explained the steps of what he was doing, and Graeme's rapt expression shouted he hung on every word.

Lexi regarded them both fondly. She was already very attached to both men, yet, at the moment, if she slipped away, neither would notice her absence.

She scanned the long tables arranged perpendicular to the double hearths. The chairs were much more ornate than what her family had in 1694, and the tables were arranged differently. More for formal setting than the more practical use of her time.

She imagined her family there, her cousin Rory pulling one of his famous pranks on his older brother, Lachlan, and her older brother, Angus shaking his head. Iain chattering away with Liam, and even herself sitting with them, in general annoyance at all her male-only cousins. Like any other shared family meal.

She'd always regretted that Brenna, her only female cousin, didn't live with them. She, like Graeme was a MacDonald, and resided at Armadale Castle. She really wasn't a blood cousin to her, Angus, or Liam, but no one ever recognized the difference.

Lexi's heart ached for the Dunvegan of her time, mixed with guilt and knowledge that she *could* return to her family at any time. If she did now, she wouldn't get to finish her own experience out on her own. Something she craved even more now that she had her chance. She wanted to shake the ideas of returning home out of her mind.

She closed the distance to an arched open doorway that also had not been present in her time, and wandered down an adjacent hallway.

There were open and closed doors on either side, and it made her think about her Aunt Claire's wide iron keyring again.

At the end of the corridor, an open double doorway led her wanderings into a sitting room. This room she remembered, because it had served the same purpose in her time. Of course, the oversized furniture was different, as well as the room's décor, but the hearth looked familiar.

The walls were painted a soft lilac and the furniture was all protected by lush velvet roping of a deep purple hue her mother would've been fond of.

So, the room was set up to be viewed, not used. The day before, Lexi had observed a group of people being led into the castle, and Graeme had remarked offhand about the people being on a tour. She'd had to act as if she'd known all about what he was referring to of course, but it'd spiked her curiosity.

Why would people want to see inside her home?

Why was this fascinating?

She whirled to leave the small room, when her eyes landed on—her own.

Lexi startled and looked the huge painting up and down. It was life-sized and housed in a dark-wood ornately carved frame, complete with gilt and flourishes. On a little bronze plaque right beneath her painted slipper-clad feet, her full Christian name was carved.

Alexandria Evelyn Claire MacLeod, 1691.

She gasped. Panic clawed at her throat. Had Graeme or James seen this painting? So close to the great hall they'd been working in every day for the past few weeks, how could they not?

The likeness was startling—there was no way the MacDonalds wouldn't recognize her in it.

Her father had hired the most famous artist in Scotland to paint it, in honor of Lexi turning eight and ten. The man had painted kings and queens, or so she'd been told.

How would she explain *this*?

Lexi looked the gorgeous feminine figure up and down. The woman in the painting was so pretty. So different than the one staring at it in true form.

The artist had softened her expression, and her ebony hair had been fashioned with woven flowers that day, left long and flowing, like her skirts.

The gown was one of the finest she owned, the same lilac matching the walls of the sitting room. It had been a gift for her naming day, as well. Her mother had insisted she wear it for the painting, but she'd argued because she'd wanted to wear the lowcut bodice dress that was a light pink shade she'd always liked. Her father had also interjected a vehement *nay* for the pink garment of choice. In the laird's opinion, it was too revealing.

She'd always hated when her usual voice-of-reason da sided with her mother against her.

Lexi snorted and shook her head. She'd been quite fashed when she'd arrived in the great hall to have her likeness recorded. That truth was nowhere in the expression of the serene lass staring out of the canvas at her, complete with a half-smile that seemed full of secrets. Her father had not been incorrect in commissioning the man. He had been good, indeed. It was exquisite.

The more she looked at her painting, the more she was convinced she was peering into a looking glass. If Graeme or his grandfather saw this piece of art, they would instantly know *she* was the lass. She couldn't pass off the nameplate as a coincidence.

Fright darted up her spine and shot into to her feet.

Lexi fled the room.

She didn't go back into the great hall where the MacDonald men worked. She wound her way outside, and eventually found herself in the gardens, a common destination after a row with her mother, when she didn't want to retreat to her rooms and embody something her mother always accused her of acting like—a child. She couldn't be caught sulking if she was outside, could she?

A sense of peace settled over her, washing away her panic over the painting and things she couldn't explain away with logic.

She took in her surroundings; greenery, budding flowers, the floral-scented air, and chirping birds. Lexi twirled, as if she had skirts to whirl around her body, and giggled at her foolish lassie-like behavior. She wanted to sprint through the pathways, but she stopped just short of emulating a bairn too much.

These gardens were much expanded than from her time, but even in 1694, Dunvegan's gardens rivaled all others in the isles. She'd always enjoyed spending time here.

"Alexandria."

She froze, and almost tripped over her own feet.

It couldn't be…

Nay.

Lexi had to swallow, then she squeezed her eyes tight, summoning all her courage before turning toward the voice she prayed she'd imagined.

Her mother stood a few feet away, flanked by Aunt Claire and her brother's wife, Lila. They were dressed simply, her mother in her signature purple, her aunt in green, and her sister-by-marriage in her favorite blue shift dress.

They looked like they always had, these three women in her family whom she loved dearly.

Lexi didn't want to see any of them, especially her former Fae princess mother.

"Thank God you're okay," Lila exclaimed, breaking away from the other two women and engulfing Lexi in a tight embrace.

"We've been worried sick," Aunt Claire echoed, cupping her face when her sister-by-marriage had released her.

"You look great!" Lila gestured to her clothing.

Lexi sucked in air so her pulse would stop pounding in her ears. Words failed her, so she didn't try to open her mouth. She met her mother's violet eyes, so like her own, and fought a shudder.

Alana regarded her regally, her expression stoic, but the emotion strong, shining from those eyes. Worry. Love.

So much disappointment.

The yoke of the thick, mixed emotions filled the air and narrowed the garden's wide stone pathway. It settled over Lexi's body, making her limbs weigh two stone each. Her chest ached. She had to fight for each breath. The woman hadn't uttered a word, other than her name.

She was torn between fleeing and throwing herself in her mother's arms, begging her forgiveness for running away.

Her aunt spoke at her side, but Lexi didn't hear her. Her sole focus was on the woman who'd given her life, the woman she'd never been able to please.

"Alexandria, let us go home," Alana said finally, extending her hand.

Her inflection had always been so different than the rest of the Clan MacLeod's Highland brogue. Her mother sounded Scottish, aye, but with a royal tone she'd been born with. Sometimes she would emulate their family — after all she'd lived in the Human Realm for years, but she was always regal when she was angry.

Was she angry now?

Or just implacable?

Either way, Lexi wasn't going to be ordered around this time. She squared her shoulders, and continued to meet her mother's gaze head-on.

"Oh, no," one of the other women muttered, but she didn't catch who.

Memory snagged her thoughts.

The high branch snapped.

Iain started to fall, and his older brothers, Lachlan and Rory, both shouted their alarm.

Lexi hadn't hesitated. She'd lifted her arm and yelled a spellword.

Iain's weight caught in the magic like a net, and it reverberated up her arm, but she had him, she would protect him.

Her little cousin had frozen midair, and she'd slowly floated him to the ground, unharmed.

Had she not used her magic, Iain would've been severely injured.

Or worse.

She had done nothing wrong, even if they'd been far outside of Dunvegan's walls.

"Nay," Lexi said. Hard. Confident.

Her mother took a few steps closer. "Nay?" She arched a delicate pale eyebrow.

"I am stayin' here."

Aunt Claire made a move, as if to step between them, but Alana raised a palm and the older woman stopped. Was she getting between them to protect Lexi from her mother, or the other way around?

At another time, Lexi might've been amused.

"It is time to go home, *mo chridhe*." Her mother's voice was even, reasonable.

"Nay, I dinnae wish ta return home." Lexi shook her head for emphasis. She hated that she already sounded defensive, petulant.

She wanted to explain that she couldn't disappear or Graeme would worry.

It was more than that, of course.

She cared for the American MacDonald, but it wasn't like she could admit to her mother she'd been in the man's bed, even if her maidenhead was still intact.

Although, Graeme and her mission to give him her innocence was only half the reason she didn't want to go home.

Lexi could be herself in this far future. She could make her own decisions. She could be the grown women her years marked her to be.

No one was lording over, telling her what she could and couldn't do. She could even use her magic—if *she* saw fit. She hadn't since she'd been there, but she could if she wanted to.

"Alexandria—"

"Nay, *mamaidh*," Lexi said in Gaelic, but it wasn't as if her mother would soften when she was being refused. "I'm needed here."

"You are needed by your family."

I will make my own family. The words were on her tongue but they would slash her mother deeply, and she didn't want to do that.

She just wanted her mother to see her for what she was; her own person.

Lexi's heart stuttered. She *could* see a family with Graeme. And James. It scared and thrilled her from the inside out. She'd known him for mere days, but it felt like years. She could see his dark eyes if she closed her own.

She couldn't tell her mother that.

"I am also needed here—"

"Graeme MacDonald is *not* your family."

She startled, physically. Wobbled on her feet, and Lila steadied her with a hand on her forearm.

Lexi glared at her mother. "Ye *dinnae* have permission ta invade my mind," she spat.

"Alana—" Aunt Claire said.

"This is none of your concern, Claire MacLeod," her mother said, without sparing her sister-by-marriage a glance.

Lexi bristled, bunching her shoulders and making tight fists at her sides. She pushed herself to her toes and grated the words out, "Aunt Claire is as important ta our *family*, as I, Mother."

Her aunt didn't look hurt by her mother's barb, instead angry. Her face was red, her mouth thinned into a hard line. Claire wasn't a pushover; she was married to a large, sometimes overbearing Highlander, and Uncle Duncan was as stubborn as they came, so she would likely be angry with Alana for some time.

Good.

Maybe the former Fae princess would apologize to someone she felt was an equal, but she never had an apology for her daughter.

"That is not true, *mo chridhe.*"

Jesu.

Not even her *thoughts* were her own.

"Get. Out. Of. My. Head." Lexi had never yelled — truly shouted — at her mother before, and it showed in her expression.

Alana's eyes went wide and her beautiful face lost its color. Her mouth hung open.

She'd shocked the woman who'd given her life.

Disrespected her in the worst way.

Lila and Claire also were obviously flabbergasted, exchanging wide glances. Neither spoke, as if they too didn't know what to say.

She imagined her mother telling her father what'd just happened; how horrible she'd been, and how disappointed he would be in her, too.

Lexi couldn't take it anymore.

"I'm stayin' *here*! I dinnae need Clan MacLeod, an' and I dinnae need *ye*!" She pushed all her hurt and anger toward her mother with the shouted words.

Her mother was an invading empath after all, and if she wanted to know what Lexi was feeling, why hold back?

Hot tears already ran down her cheeks before she whirled away and started running. She couldn't see, but she didn't care.

Until she ran smack into someone, before she'd even left the gardens.

"Och, lassie. Do ye wanna tell me what tha' was all abou'?" Warm, weathered hands settled at her elbows, steadying her.

Heart still thundering from her throat, Lexi blinked to clear her vision and looked up into the dark eyes of James MacDonald.

chapter thirteen

▶▶ **W**here's Graeme?" Lexi sniffled and wiped the last of the tears from her face, as she walked to the closest bench beside James MacDonald.

After the elderly man had found her in the gardens, she hadn't been able to find her voice and answer his query.

What would she say, anyway?

"The lad is doin' somethin' fer me," he said, as if that explained everything.

His hip must've been bothering him because he was plodding along with a light limp, but she'd never point it out.

"Are ye hungry, lass?" James offered her a brown sack and slid onto the wooden bench, with a slight wince.

She shook her head and took a seat beside him. Lexi studied his profile. His face was so much like Graeme's, the same cheekbones, the same dark eyes. His silver hair was short and neat, making his bushy eyebrows seem out of place.

He didn't speak again, although she could feel he'd caught her close observation.

Lexi was drawn to his stoic peace, and was again

reminded of her own grandfather. She'd grieved so hard when he'd passed. "I lost my grandfa," she blurted.

"Sorry ta hear that, lass." He opened the bag he'd offered her moments before and pulled out a smaller item, also wrapped in paper, but it was ivory in color. Soon, he'd opened the wrapping and revealed a sandwich.

Lexi had eaten one yesterday for midday meal. The concoction of bread with meat and cheese inside was new to her, one she'd liked very much.

She couldn't eat now because she was still too shaken from the run-in with her mother.

Where had her mother, aunt and sister-by-marriage gone?

She hadn't even gotten a chance to tell Aunt Claire that she'd tasted coffee, and how much she liked it, or the unwelcome feeling of wearing a bra for the first time. There was so much she wanted to talk to them about.

Would they go back to 1694 and leave her be?

Lexi shuddered. Her mother wasn't used to having to back down; nor did the former princess usually give up. She'd hurt her intentionally with the words she'd flung.

Guilt swirled low in her gut, mixed with regret. She loved her mother. She loved her family.

She'd declared the opposite, but she really only wanted them to stop smothering her.

Lexi had been so angry when her mother had pushed into her head and read her thoughts without permission, just like the day she'd left home.

What was she supposed to do next?

If she could center herself and concentrate, she might be able to tell if they were still close — or at least in the same time — through her magic, but she was nowhere calm enough for that to work now.

Lexi doubted her mother would truly admit defeat.

"Does that mean yer memories are back?" James asked as he bit into the sandwich. He was looking at his food, not at her, but it didn't matter.

It was as if he was looking straight through her again.

Lexi startled on the edge of the bench, and her cheeks seared. She couldn't look at Graeme's grandfather.

"Unless..."

She managed to throw him a glance, but couldn't make the eye contact last. "Un...un...less?" she stuttered out.

"Ye never lost yer memories a'tall?" He casually chewed, then took another bite of the sandwich. He pulled a bottle of water from the brown sack, unscrewed the cap, took a swig, then replaced it. Offered her the bottle.

Lexi shook her head. Chaos danced across her mind. She opened her mouth to speak, but no sound came out.

James looked at her again, his dark eyes compelling her maintain the eye contact. His gaze was soft and kind, and made her tear up all over again.

Her bottom lip trembled, so she bit down to make it stop. Her eyes stung and one tear rolled down her cheek when Graeme's grandfather spoke again.

"The paintin' in the purple sittin' room at the end of

the corridor." It wasn't a question; it was a statement.

"'Tis me," Lexi blurted.

James nodded and took the last bite of his sandwich, as if she hadn't just admitted something impossible. Admitted to time travel, and he wasn't even the least bit shocked. "Thought as much."

"I traveled through time. From the year of our lord, sixteen hundred and ninety-four."

Again, he nodded, as if they discussed the weather. "Is the lad aware?"

She shook her head and swiped her cheeks.

James made a noise, as if he was mulling that over. "The lasses in the garden?" he asked after a few heartbeats of silence.

"My mother, aunt, and my brother's wife."

Again, only a mere nod.

"Ye dinnae want ta go back?"

"It's…complicated," Lexi whispered, offering a phrase she'd heard Graeme tell someone on the little black rectangle. She'd learned from conversations it was called a cellphone, or as James called it, a mobile phone.

Not only was it for communication, it was a font of information about everything and anything. It, too, seemed like magic. Perhaps it was the modern times' form of magic, different than Fae magic, but magic, nonetheless.

Graeme's grandfather threw her a smirk that took years off his weathered face. He took another sip of water from the bottle and licked his lips. His expression was pensive, as if he gathered his thoughts. "Yer mother, lassie?"

"Is Fae," she supplied, her heart skipping a few beats. The back of her neck was hot, and warmth crept into her cheeks until they were aflame, all the way up to her ears. She'd just said something aloud she'd been raised to *never* reveal to someone outside the family, let alone to someone with James' surname. She squirmed in her seat, her stomach somersaulting.

"Yer father?"

Lexi cocked her head to one side. That was probably the last thing she'd expected him to ask. Just like with her other revelations, Graeme's grandfather took her confessions in stride, accepting her at her word.

"He's..." she had to clear her throat and start again. "The current Laird MacLeod, in my time. His name is Alex."

"Ah, so yer named fer him."

She nodded.

Graeme's grandfather's expression was still so placid and accepting, mixed with some of the same thoughtfulness.

"Yer...yer...no' surprised?"

"The Faery Folk have always been real ta me, lassie." He patted her knee and offered the softest smile.

Lexi's eyes smarted as she again flashed back to her own grandfather, Iain MacLeod. Although his eyes had been blue, the opposite of James', they'd always held the same kindness and love for her.

She would've also wagered her father's favorite pocket watch that Graeme had never seen that particular expression on his grandfather's visage.

Lexi whimpered and threw her arms around James

MacDonald.

He gathered her to him without hesitation, and held her close. The older man smelled of old wood and oil and it made her think of her father's ledger room. Comfort and safety.

"Thank ye," she whispered.

A few heartbeats of a companionable silence passed, then Graeme's grandfather gently released her, and got to his feet. "Break's over. Back ta work."

chapter fourteen

►► "I've been looking everywhere for you guys," Graeme said, throwing his hands up as the pair walked in from outside. He stood next to their small work area, after he'd been back from the errand for Gramps for what felt like forever.

When he'd gotten back to the great hall of the big castle, Lexi and Gramps had been nowhere in sight. He'd gone up and down all the close hallways, peeked in every open room, then outside again. He'd given up and come back to their work area.

He'd grabbed food for him and Lexi, but it'd long gone cold. His grandfather always brought a sandwich from home, and had always turned down offers for a hot meal from the closest pub.

Gramps grumbled a non-response including something that sounded like, "lunch," then something in Gaelic.

Without sparing him another glance, the older man resumed his seat at the hearth—but at least the curmudgeon had agreed to sit. He'd have to shift later, to go lower, but it was a good concession for now.

Graeme chided himself for the mean thought about his grandfather. Gramps had been...well, *nice* all morning. Had actually showed him techniques, and he'd reveled in it. James MacDonald had even listened to his input, and Graeme had been able to show off some of his own knowledge.

It'd felt foreign and damn good.

Why now, why today, he could never guess, but he just wanted it to go on, so they could be a true team. It was all he'd ever wanted.

He glanced at Lexi, and froze.

Her gorgeous face was flushed pink and her eyes were swollen and red, as if she'd been crying.

Any idea of asking her if she was hungry for lunch dissolved, the white paper bags on the small table near their workspace forgotten.

Graeme was at her side in seconds. "What happened?" he demanded.

Surprise darted across those violet eyes and she shook her head, making her ebony locks dance over her shoulders. "No-nothin'." The lie made her turn even more crimson back to her ears.

"Leave the lass be," his grandfather commanded from the hearth.

Graeme looked from one to the other, and frowned.

"What's going on?" he asked.

"Are ye here ta work, lad?" Gramps barked. Now, he was back to the old, critical grouch again. So much for the progress they'd made today.

"Aye, I am," he said, but looked at his little foundling.

She smirked, probably at his word choice.

What the hell had happened?

Had his grandfather made his lover cry?

"Then do so," Gramps gestured to the double hearth, a tool in hand. The master restorer then resumed his work, apparently tuning them out as he focused on his task.

Graeme didn't move right away. He didn't want to leave Lexi's side, despite his desire to learn from the master. Something had obviously upset her, and he needed to know, *now*.

So he could promptly kill it—err, fix it.

Make her smile again.

His gut wobbled and his heart stuttered.

What was this woman doing to him?

"Go on," she whispered, gesturing toward the double hearth. She offered a smile, but it had a wobble to it that made him want to kiss her.

He cupped her face and made her meet his eyes. "Lexi, what's wrong?"

She shook her head and made the smile wider, but he didn't buy it.

Lexi gently pushed his fingers away. "If ye dinnae get back at it, the teachin' will ne'er continue."

Graeme sighed. She was as stubborn as his grandfather. However, she was also right. He wanted to seize the man's rare generosity, and learn what he could. He also wanted to show his grandfather what *he* was capable of, too.

He dropped a kiss on her cheek and nodded, then joined his grandfather at the hearth. "You'll tell me later." It wasn't a question.

She nodded, and it was a small thing he could almost feel the denial roll off of, despite the acquiescence of the gesture.

Lexi had no intention of telling him what'd happened to cause the tears, but he'd argue with her about it later.

Graeme studied his grandfather's profile. He didn't look weak or injured, or even old. The man looked like the skilled master craftsman he was, like he'd worked on thousands of historical landmarks as easily as breathing—and he probably had.

James MacDonald was completely enveloped by what he was doing, but the man had more than a stubborn streak. He was made of the stuff, so there would be no point to Graeme asking his grandfather to spill the beans about what happened with Lexi. The man wouldn't utter a word about it.

On the contrary, they'd team up to shut him out.

What kind of shit was that?

Over the past two days of having Lexi with them at Dunvegan, his grandfather had welcomed her, talked with her often, minus the gruff edge he gave to Graeme, and maybe even Bridget—although the curvy redhead could get the man to listen better than he could. Even with his assistant, Gramps was rough around the edges.

Lexi, on the other hand, had melted the old man, if only a little.

Graeme admired her for it, and saw a tenderness no one could have convinced him of James MacDonald was even capable of.

Had Gramps been like that with his wife?

Sadly, Graeme's grandmother had died when his father was a boy, so he'd never gotten the chance to meet her.

His grandfather had always been gruff with him, too, even back during his childhood when he'd been convinced he'd die of boredom on the Isle of Skye without his video games.

Graeme smiled to himself, but with a tinge of regret.

He'd misused that time. He should've thrown himself into Gramps' trade back then, but it wasn't like he'd known he'd wanted to follow the man's footsteps. Nor had he known he'd lose his parents.

Doesn't matter now.

He chided himself to get to work, before James could realize he still stood around and bark at him. Graeme didn't want to lose the progress they'd made that day, so he'd grip it with both hands, and hold onto it for as long as he could.

Lexi stayed in the great hall, half-afraid if she wandered Dunvegan, she'd run into her mother, Aunt Claire and Lila again. She was calmer now, perhaps because of the admission to the older MacDonald, or just being near Graeme helped soothe her nerves.

If she concentrated, she could use her magic to sense if her family was still in the current century, but she didn't want to.

She didn't want to know; she didn't want to think about staying or going.

She wanted it all to go away.

If her guilt regarding staying with Graeme had been

bothering her before, it was a living thing now, threatening to consume her whole, but not because she hadn't gone home at her mother's demand.

Lexi had *yelled* at her mother.

She'd declared she didn't need her.

She blinked away a new round of tears and forced her eyes on the two MacDonalds from the future, both of whom she cared for greatly.

They were speaking in low tones, both calm and involved in their task.

"Like that?" Graeme asked his grandfather.

The older man nodded and gave the barest hint of a smile.

She smiled, too.

They were getting along famously, as Aunt Claire would say, and it was a wonder to watch them work.

The look on her lover's face was one of grateful worship, mixed with concentration, and she could feel his sense of accomplishment, and it warmed her heart.

However, it also made the muscle in her chest ache, because of the words she'd flung at her mother. Sensing or feeling what another was feeling was only another reminder of the woman who'd given her life.

Lexi wanted to apologize. She needed to. Owed the former princess that.

The argument from the day she'd run away seemed to pale in comparison to what'd happened that day in the gardens, but she'd been wrong in both instances.

She shouldn't have left.

She should've faced the situation and talked it out with her family.

Using magic in the open *was* dangerous, no matter her intentions and the relief that her little cousin remained unharmed.

If Lexi thought she and her mother had had problems before, that was now amplified, since she'd meant to hurt her with what she'd said.

Lexi *had* meant to hurt Alana.

What she'd said wasn't true.

She *did* need her mother, and her family, for that matter. She needed their love.

However, just because she needed them, it didn't mean she couldn't make her own choices, too. They needed to recognize she was an adult and capable of handling her own life. Especially, her mother. Her father, too, for that matter.

In the very least, they would know she wasn't lost or in danger. She was safe with Graeme—even if her father and Uncle Duncan would protest that he was a MacDonald.

Lexi closed her eyes briefly and sucked in a calming breath.

How much of a reprieve would her mother give her?

She wanted Alana and any other family members to remain in 1694.

Lexi sighed and slipped away from the work area. She studied each wall of the great hall, each painting, each decorative element, comparing them to what they looked like in her time. Despite the differences, the place felt like Dunvegan.

Home.

Her eyes smarted for the hundredth time that day, and Lexi glanced over her shoulder at her two MacDonald men.

They still worked and talked, James teaching, and Graeme learning. Working in tandem as a real team. Working like they were smoothing over their normal tension, building a real relationship.

She wanted to fix things with her mother. Truly.

Lexi just wasn't done in this time. She wasn't done with Graeme and James.

Would she ever be done with Graeme?

Her heart ached a protest, and stuttered before returning to a normal rhythm.

She wouldn't ever be done with her MacDonald from the future.

Eventually, she'd have to go home, wouldn't she?

She shook herself physically, wiggling her shoulders, and straightening her spine.

She needed to banish it all from her head, and her heart. The situation would force her to handle it eventually, but later. When she had to.

Graeme called to her, and she threw a smile over her shoulder for the man that made her insides mush.

Lexi dashed back to the hearth and the man she couldn't bear to leave—yet.

Ever, whispered in the back of her mind, but she pushed it away, too and concentrated on his midnight eyes assessing her again.

She still had to convince him to make love to her, so her plans to stay would continue. She was on a mission of sorts, and she promptly ignored the, *then what?* that popped into her head, too.

Her parents sure as hell—to quote Aunt Claire—would be opposed to her little goal, no matter how old she was. It would be just another disappointment.

Lexi couldn't let that bother her.

It was all for later.

It *had* to be.

chapter fifteen

exi flashed Graeme a brilliant grin and grabbed the wheel of Gramps' blue truck with both overeager slender hands.

His heart actually fluttered at her open, carefree expression, and he hollered at himself to get it together — an overly familiar sentiment since he'd found this beautiful young woman on the rocky beach just over a week ago.

He cleared his throat so he could get words out. "Are you sure you want to do this?"

Lexi nodded, those violet eyes bright. "Aye. 'Tis like riding a horse, nay?"

He laughed. "Well, not at all, really. But I haven't ridden a horse since I was a kid."

"I love ta ride," she said, her words holding some palpable, nostalgic sense. "I miss Turadh somethin' fierce." Her gorgeous cheeks darkened, and she bit her bottom lip.

"Turadh?" Graeme repeated, likely slaughtering the pronunciation of the Gaelic name.

She remained quiet for a few seconds and she wouldn't look at him.

"Lexi?" he ventured, tugging on her pale blue short-sleeve to keep things light.

She wore a blue and white baseball style tee, paired with the same dark jeans she loved — and he loved her in. Her ass had been made for tight jeans.

He wanted her to smile again, like she had moments before, lively, excited and innocent.

Her throat worked when she finally spared him a glance, but no words were born.

"Did you remember something?" he asked gently.

Since he'd found her, she often had slips just like this. When he'd ask, she always denied any actual memory or shoved the idea away with things he assumed she thought he'd want to hear.

The date next week circled on the calendar loomed — the appointment he was supposed to take her back to Dr. Guinn for a checkup. More than likely, the physician would want to proceed with an MRI.

The day he'd found her, Graeme would've never allowed it, but now, it seemed like the thing to do, right?

She couldn't have endured it that day.

Could she now?

What had changed?

Maybe her subconscious coughed up random memories, but Lexi claimed she couldn't place it.

Something whispered in the back of his mind that he didn't know the whole truth, but he discarded it, as always when he latched onto the idea that she wasn't being honest with him.

He didn't like it. So he didn't want to face that she could be lying.

Lexi wasn't lying, was she?

Why would she have a reason to lie about amnesia?

Did she not trust him, after everything they'd gone through? After all their nights together?

The whole concept was silly.

"Lexi?" Graeme prompted again when she still neglected to answer.

"I think I had a horse. Named Turadh." Her cheeks were bright red, but at least she was looking at him.

"A horse? That's great. What else can you recall?"

She shook her head, and her pretty eyes went hazy with unshed tears.

He sighed. He felt like an asshole again, although he shouldn't, and follow-up questions were only natural, but he still called himself a few choice names. Rushing things in her condition was never helpful.

"C'mere," he whispered and tugged her into his arms.

Lexi didn't hesitate, and holding her felt as right as it always did.

She snuggled into his chest and tucked her face into his neck. Her warm breath kissing his skin made him shiver in a good way.

She'd slept in his bed the night before, like every night since the first she'd spent in his little cottage. Lexi continued to test him, pushing him to take her virginity. Rushing that pivotal moment Lexi had seemed more than willing.

He'd held her, kissed her, gave her pleasure, let her give him pleasure, including a few blow jobs, but Graeme couldn't bring himself to be the first man to push inside her, although he fucking wanted to. He was burning to take her. Orgasms or not, what they'd done wasn't as good as full-blown sex.

Sex with Lexi would be the most amazing sex he'd ever had in his life. Everything he'd already experienced with her told him that much.

"I'm sorry for pushing you," he whispered into her soft hair.

She smelled like his shampoo, and it make him smile.

"Nay, I'm sorry," she whispered into his chest. "I dinnae remember…I…"

"Shhh, don't worry about it, okay?" Graeme dropped a kiss on her head, then on her lips when Lexi tilted away to look at him.

He kept it short and chaste. Then pulled away, because if he didn't, they would be making out in his grandfather's truck like teens doing something wrong in about two seconds flat.

One kiss and he was a goner.

Lexi offered a small tremulous smile.

He wiped the moisture from her cheeks and cupped her face. "You'll remember in time, no matter how long it takes. Stay with me until then. Stay with me as long as you want." *Always,* wanted to tack itself onto the end of his statement, but Graeme shoved it away. It wasn't his right, no matter how perfect she felt in his arms.

Her smile grew. Her purple eyes were fathomless, like he could slip into them and never find his way out.

His gut jumped, because he didn't want to fight that sentiment. He *did* want her to stay with him always. Forever, or whatever.

It wasn't possible.

He knew nothing about her.

She knew nothing about her.

Why, after a week, had no one come looking for her?

They'd even called the authorities to see if anyone had reported someone fitting Lexi's description as a missing person. Not one.

Nothing made sense when it came to his little foundling, including the way she made him feel about her.

Graeme kissed her forehead because he couldn't help himself.

Lexi smiled again, tenderly.

It took all he was made of not to nix the driving lesson and drag her back into his cottage, change his mind about being her first, and make love to her all damn day long. It was Saturday and he was free of work and Gramps. What a way to spend the day. Talk about perfect.

He cleared his throat, because he wasn't sure he could speak, otherwise. "Well, are you ready to do this?" He'd backed the truck from his normal spot in front of the cottage and had it facing the road, so all she'd have to do was pull out straight.

Lexi nodded with the same eagerness of before, and flexed her long slender fingers on the wheel.

Graeme couldn't tear his eyes from her hands, or stop remembering what her touch felt like all over his body.

He needed to focus.

Get your head out of the gutter, dammit.

"What's first?" she asked, her brogue rolling over

him like a physical touch.

He could be her first. He only needed to say the word.

Graeme took a breath when his cock jumped. He cleared his throat—again—and met her violet gaze. "Turn the key, like I showed you—oh, put your seatbelt on first." He did the same, hoping it would snap him into the driving lesson and get his head—and his dick—out of his bedroom, with her naked in his arms.

Lexi's expression was so intense with concentration, and her little pink tongue stuck out from the corner of her mouth. She turned the key already in the truck's ignition. The engine roared to life, as ready to go as his lover was.

Graeme smiled and adjusted his shoulders against the passenger seat. He didn't need to notice that tongue of hers or remember what it could do to his body, or he would really be sporting a boner in the truck.

"Okay, pull the shifter toward you and down two notches to the *D*, that's for *Drive*."

Lexi didn't speak, but when she pulled on the handle sticking out of the side of the steering column, it didn't move, and her nervous eyes landed on him.

"A little harder, darlin'. Do you want me to do it?"

Harder.

Bad choice of words.

Oh, shut up, you perv.

"Nay," she said, determination wrapping the word and making him laugh. She hesitated before trying again.

Graeme smiled, also just as resolute to ignore his

inner monologue. "Let's do it together. Make sure your foot is on the break, like I showed you, okay?"

"'Tis." Lexi nodded.

When he covered her smaller hand with his on the shifter, a shot of awareness went down his spine and landed on his crotch.

Oh. Shit.

Graeme took a subtle breath. Maybe he should take her virginity, make love to her a few times, until the innocent temptress was out of his system, because his body's constant reaction to simple, non-sexual touches was getting ridiculous.

He cleared his throat for the millionth time that day, and pulled the shifter toward her and down. "See? Feel it? It'll lock in there, and then we're in gear."

"Aye," she said, but she was looking at the road and not him.

That was probably for the better.

The truck didn't move or shift forward, and Lexi threw him a look, her brow drawn tight in obvious confusion.

"Your foot's on the break, darlin'. Give it some gas." Graeme gave her a small smile of encouragement and it was the most difficult thing in the world to pull his hand back, to stop touching her. "Tap it, don't lay on it."

Every single one of his damn driving instructions had a sexual connotation.

Tap it. Feel it. Lock it in. Lay on it. Even *give it some gas.*

He was in so much trouble.

Or he was just a pervert destined for hell.

Lexi did as he'd said, and flashed a million-watt

smile when the truck surged forward.

He laughed again when the motor hummed and they slowed. "Do it again, slow and steady. If you take your foot off, we'll slow but we won't stop unless you break. Be careful, but you got this."

She nodded, such purpose in her expression again.

They made it down the street and back a few times, and Graeme taught her how to turn the big vehicle carefully.

Lexi was a natural, and followed directions well. She had them cruising at about forty MPH — about sixty-three kilometers, Scottish-speak — at the fastest, and her hair blew in the wind from the open windows. She grinned from ear-to-ear and it did funny things to his insides.

She was so damn gorgeous.

"See? I bet you drove before, and it's just something you needed to remember, like everything else."

Her joy fell off a bit and she shrugged. "Maybe," she whispered, but her expression was guarded.

Graeme squeezed her knee and let it go. They were having such a good time; he didn't want her to get sad or cry again.

"Can we go again?" Lexi asked, breaking the tiny silence. One of the corners of her delectable mouth shot up, and he had to shake himself away the temptation to lick her there.

"Of course. Turn slowly, and go out onto the road."

When she pulled the truck back into his usual parking place in front of the small cottage fifteen minutes later, Lexi's pretty face was lit up with a sense of accomplishment Graeme could almost feel.

He chuckled and caressed her cheek. "You did great, darlin'."

She smiled and pulled the keys from the ignition, then they slid out of the pickup at the same time.

"Can I drive on the morrow?" she asked, as she met him at the hood, dropping the jangling bundle into his waiting palm.

He didn't stop to consider her odd choice of words. Sometimes Lexi said things that were old-sounding, but he was getting used to it. He hit the lock button on the fob, then pocketed the keys.

"Sure, I don't see why not."

She squealed and threw herself into his arms.

Graeme caught her up and took a step back so they both wouldn't land on the ground — although the idea of her on top of him wasn't a bad one.

He hadn't been expecting her to throw her weight at him, but his arms went around her at the same time Lexi wound hers around his neck.

Kissing her was as natural as breathing. Her lips were heading for his anyway, so he deepened things and tasted her. Like he'd wanted to all day. Like he hadn't had a drink of water in days.

Their tongues danced and dueled, and she fought him for control like she always did. Desire shot low, hot and immediate. He was hard already, and his pulse thundered in his ears.

Graeme tore his mouth away. "Let's take this inside," he panted.

Lexi nodded, but her cheeks pinked, her mouth

plump and begging for more.

They stumbled inside, still kissing and touching, and he managed to kick the door shut behind them. She was on him again before he could hit the light switch.

Her mouth moved under his as if she was an expert seductress, but he could sense, maybe taste, her innocence. It was always there when he kissed her. It was as appealing as she was.

A virgin she might've admitted to being, but her passion and interest in what they were about to do covered any obvious nerves she might have.

Then again, from the first night at his place, the first time Lexi had crawled into his bed and told him she hadn't wanted to be alone; she hadn't really been all that shy. She'd always kissed him back, fervently, passionately, making his blood boil.

Graeme slid his hands down her back and cupped her perfect ass in the tight denim. It was round and high, just the right amount of muscle, and she tightened that toned flesh as he kneaded. A groan slipped out, but she swallowed it as she rubbed her tongue against his.

Lexi was as aggressive as he was, and he freakin' loved it. Of course, they might not have gone all the way, but they'd spent days getting to know each other's bodies.

Now, hers was as familiar as her touch. He may have told her it wasn't his place to take her virginity, and he might still feel a smidge of guilt over the idea, but she hadn't felt wrong from the start—maybe even as far back as the innocent kiss in the truck when he'd found her on the beach.

Over the nights she'd spent in his bed, he'd taught her how he liked to be touched, and Graeme had certainly enjoyed every inch of her lithe little body.

Lexi screamed when she came, and he got off on that, too, his ability to make her writhe and call his name when she tumbled over the edge. The look on her face in those moments was intense and made him even hotter. His cock throbbed, the zipper of his jeans taking a bite, despite the cotton of his boxer briefs.

Damn, his blood sizzled, making his head even hazier with desire. If he didn't slow things down, he was going to come. Before he was even freed from denim. In his pants, as if *he* was the virgin.

Why was he so close to losing control?

They'd done this before, this preamble of passion, after all. They hadn't even made it all the way to his bedroom yet, he needed to calm the hell down.

Graeme had told her it didn't feel right to take her virginity, but she kept pushing him. How much longer could he refuse her?

Hell, he didn't want to.

He wanted her.

This was the natural culmination of things, wasn't it?

He could try to talk himself out of it all he wanted. He could say it was the age difference, the amnesia, the fact they hadn't found her family after a week, but would any of that really stop him?

It was all chatter, slinking to the back of his head as he let his hormones rule.

Graeme wrenched away from her delicious kiss,

panting through the fuzziness in his head and begging his eyes to focus so he could concentrate enough to form words. "Lexi, we need to slow down..."

One look at her face revved him up all over again, and he'd never been harder in his life.

His dick *hurt*.

Lexi's alabaster skin was flushed pink up to her ears, a bright streak of color splashed over her high cheekbones and the bridge of her pert little nose. Her lips were kiss-swollen and crimson. When her little rosebud tongue darted out to moisten the bottom one, Graeme's erection pulsed, as if there was a string connecting her mouth to his engorged head.

Her small breasts rose and fell as she too struggled for normal breath, and didn't he want to rip off the blue and white Henley she'd gotten the day they'd gone to Flora' shop.

He swallowed. Twice.

Big violet eyes locked onto his, but they were misty, so much passion there he wanted to nix the slow plan and toss her to his bed.

She wouldn't say no.

Therein lay the problem.

"Graeme..."

His name on Lexi's lips in her brogue was going to be his undoing.

"I want this. I want ye. I've already tol' ye." Each word was delayed by ragged breathing that just made him hotter and hotter.

She might be a virgin, but he'd never had a more responsive lover. The nights of *almost* hadn't been satisfying enough, despite the orgasms on both their parts.

Even though he'd always been the one to put on the breaks, telling her over and over he couldn't take her virginity, that it wasn't right he was the one.

Lexi kept declaring she wanted to give it to him, that she wanted him, just like she'd declared again now.

Damn, she had him teetering on the edge of control, but it was something he should be used to by now. He'd been a fool to let the foreplay continue for over a week.

The word *culmination* popped into his mind again, like it had earlier, and he raked his eyes over her gorgeous flushed face again, watched her small high breasts heave against tight cotton. His heart skipped.

He was an idiot to think he could've stopped *this*.

Graeme couldn't stop touching her. Holding her.

Fuck if he could stop kissing her.

He wanted her.

She wanted him.

Kept telling him to take her.

He was a man, wasn't he?

There were limits to his control, no matter his best intentions.

Fuck him; Graeme had never wanted a woman more than he wanted Lexi.

Maybe if she wasn't a virgin, he'd have less guilt, but the idea of him being her first sure as hell didn't lessen his want. If anything, it drove him. *He* would be the first to touch her this way, the first to be *inside* her.

He honest-to-God gulped.

Because he might come in his jeans after all.

Did Lexi's amnesia effect what they were doing? Would it affect what they were about to do?

What if she was married and she didn't remember?

The thought punched him low in the gut, hard.

Sure, he wanted her, but sex was sex. It wouldn't be more between them. As soon as they found her family, figured her out, she'd leave, right?

Even if Graeme took her virginity, it wasn't like she'd end up with him.

Marry *him*.

He shook his head.

"What?" Lexi's question was low…and hurt. Obvious pain glinted in those eyes and crossed her gorgeous face.

She'd misinterpreted his gesture.

Get the hell out of your head, and get with *her.*

"Oh, that wasn't for you, darlin'. That was me…talking to me, I guess."

She arched a slender eyebrow, but she didn't look hurt anymore. "Do ye want me, Graeme?"

Did he ever.

"Aye." He smirked with the use of her word, and it melted into a genuine smile when her gorgeous face relaxed even more.

chapter sixteen

a^{*ye.*}

Graeme's single word lit Lexi up inside.

Triumph rolled over her. Of course, he'd admitted to wanting her before, but somehow this was hotter, faster, felt like more.

Graeme wouldn't deny her this time.

Graeme would take her.

Lexi would give him her innocence.

Now, in fact.

He'd already touched her like no one had ever done. She couldn't imagine wanting to be with another man. Graeme had kissed and licked up and down her entire body, including in her most private places—something she hadn't even known a man could do to a woman.

That had been how she'd experienced her first orgasm, and it had been glorious. Lexi had wanted more then, and she wanted more now.

She wanted *all* of him.

"Take me ta yer bed, Graeme MacDonald."

"This is so not a good idea," he muttered on a groan, but he kissed her again, and Lexi clung to him, caressing his back and tight rear end.

She'd seen him fully naked, felt him as such against her own naked body, in his bed and in the shower, but he'd made it clear in every instance that he would show her pleasure without that last step, and it had made her want him even more.

Graeme swept her up into his arms without breaking their latest kiss and Lexi moaned into his mouth.

She wove her arms around his neck and held on tight.

He set her to the center of his bed so gently, so opposite of the heat building between them, her heart melted even more for her American from the far future.

She wanted to cling to him, hold onto him forever.

Graeme pulled away only to shuck his red shirt with the MacDonald name on it, and Lexi took the time to push her socks and shoes off her feet. They *thudded* to the wood-planked floor.

She shimmed out of her jeans and pink nickers and tossed them across the room. Her blue and white leine was next, and lastly the uncomfortable brassiere. She'd obeyed Flora's instructions and worn it beneath every one of her new modern leines, but she didn't like it at all. It was uncomfortable and restricting, and she still preferred a proper corset or the tight bodice of a gown. She flung the bra down.

Lexi was naked in his bed.

Waiting.

She pushed to her elbows and their gazes collided.

Graeme stood by his bed, his powerful chest heaving as he took a breath, then another. His muscles rippled and her fingers itched to play in the sparse hair dotting his pectorals. He still wore his jeans, but his feet were bare.

He crawled onto the bed and hovered over her, but he didn't touch or kiss her.

"Graeme —"

"Lexi —"

They spoke at the same time. Stared at each other for a few heartbeats.

His handsome face was flushed from their kisses, his sandy locks mussed, and Lexi wanted to taste his mouth again. Touch him all over.

Have him inside her.

Finally.

"Dinnae deny me," she whispered. Even to her own ears, her statement was half-plea, half-demand. Her heart ached at the thought that he might set her aside yet again.

Graeme ran his hand through his hair, making his shaggy locks even more of a mess.

She loved it. Wanted to run her fingers through it, too.

"Lexi, I want you to be sure about this. Once you give yourself to someone for the first time, you can't do it again. You will no longer be a virgin. You only ever have *one* first time. It will always have been with me."

Her heart tripped. She'd already told him that was exactly what she wanted, and it was. "I've already given myself ta ye," she whispered. "So, yer already my first, as ye say."

The apple of his throat bobbed as her lover swallowed. "I...guess you're...right."

"My first kiss," Lexi said. She sat up, coming closer

to his face. "My first touch." She cupped his cheek, then ran two fingers down his chest and was pleased by his physical reaction; Graeme shuddered and the tent at the apex of his thighs seemed to tighten, become more prominent.

She moved even closer, pushing to her knees, until their lips were millimeters apart, and she reveled in his hot breath on her mouth. "The first man to touch me here." She put one of his hands to her breast. Her nipple tightened when his skin touched hers. "And here." She dragged his fingers down her belly, and a tremor racked *her* frame when she brushed her sex, even if she was the one guiding his hand.

Graeme made a noise that was half-growl, half-groan and lunged forward, grabbed her shoulders and covered her lips with his.

He kissed her until her head spun and her body threatened to combust. He kissed her until Lexi felt completely possessed by him, but she didn't care.

It was she wanted. What she'd begged for.

She wanted to belong to Graeme MacDonald *completely.*

He broke away on a pant and met her eyes again. "One last chance to have an out…" Each word he pushed out was delayed from the one before it by ragged breaths.

"I dinnae seek an ou'." Lexi reached for the fly on his pants and tugged the button open, then pushed the zipper down.

Zippers were so much easier than the ties or buttons she was used to, and she liked them very much since arriving in the future. Especially when they allowed quick access to the flesh she sought.

She shoved her hand inside his short pants — which he'd told her were called boxer briefs — and gripped his hard length. He was so warm in her fingers, so firm, yet his skin was soft, responsive. She enjoyed stroking him.

"Lexi —" Her name on his lips was choked and he jerked in her grip. "Do you want me to finish what we started the way you want?"

Their gazes met, and Graeme wore a sexy smirk.

"Aye."

"Then let me go, or I'm gonna come in my pants."

She giggled and kissed him, but her lover pulled away, gently disengaging from her touch. With quick movements, he shed his jeans and boxer briefs and joined her in his bed, finally as naked as she.

They reached for each other at the same time, and Lexi kissed him again, getting as close to his chest as she could. She wanted his weight on top of her, wanted him inside her finally.

"I'll make it good for you, Lexi." His dark eyes were so intense, she couldn't look away.

"Ye...ye always make it good, Graeme," she whispered.

He smiled, and it was a soft tender thing that made her heart skip. "Glad you think so, but I want to make sure you don't hurt. The first time hurts for a woman."

Her mother had explained such, but it didn't change her mind. Lexi had been in his bed for over a week now, and Graeme had only made her feel bliss. She wasn't afraid that he'd hurt her.

"We just need to make sure you're wet enough, but you usually get wet for me."

She shivered because she understood exactly what he meant.

Graeme often spoke low nothings about wanting to touch her, taste her, and where he would do so. Although she didn't always know to what he was referring, the words increased the desire for his kisses and caresses. It made her burn for him even more that she could make him crazy, as he'd told her on more than one occasion.

He urged her to lie on the bed, and held himself above her. He cupped her breasts and she whimpered.

Lexi's nipples were already hard and aching for him, even before he enclosed his hot mouth around one, while gently kneading the other with talented fingers. She wiggled beneath him, needing his touch and his mouth lower.

Graeme chuckled. "Always so demanding," he murmured against her ribcage, but he didn't disappoint, or make her wait. He kissed and licked his way down her belly, nipping her hips and caressing the backs of her thighs.

"More," she moaned, lifting her bottom, and opening wider for him. What the man could do with his tongue between her legs made her eyes roll back into her head until she saw stars and shouted her pleasure.

"Whatever my lady wants," he said right before swiping his tongue against the bundle of nerves at the top of her sex.

She screamed his name, and buried her hand in his

thick sandy locks. Lexi's thighs already shook even before Graeme sucked her into his mouth. She threw back her head, pressing into the pillows. Tugging on his hair wasn't enough, she needed to hold onto something to steady her.

He slid a finger inside her, rubbing and thrusting gingerly, but he gave her his free hand.

Lexi entwined their fingers, right as ecstasy rolled over her in waves. Her inner muscles clenched, contracting and relaxing; sending her over the edge with a rush of delicious sensations. Climax hit hard and fast and she moaned his name over and over.

Her whole body quaked, and he stroked her inner thigh as she came down from the orgasm.

"Damn, darlin', that was the fastest I've ever made you come." He pressed a kiss to her pelvis, right above her sex, and flashed a grin.

"Graeme…" she breathed.

His dark eyes danced when their gazes locked, but he sucked in a sharp breath and suddenly got serious. Her lover shot up her body, tugging her to his chest between heartbeats.

Graeme's mouth settled over hers again, and Lexi tasted her own essence on his tongue. It wasn't unpleasant; on the contrary, it made her overheated again, setting her blood to a rolling boil. The throb between her legs was no longer one of satiation, it was an ache of need. Only he could fill the empty void inside her.

He kissed her until her head spun and she needed to pant to bring air in. Without breaking their lip-lock, he rolled them over until Graeme lay flat on the soft bed and she straddled his hips, her knees on either side of him.

Lexi rubbed her breasts into his chest, and he groaned.

He caressed her back in long strokes as they kissed.

Reaching between their bodies, she gripped his manhood, pumping him a few times, until he lifted his hips and her fingers cupped his heavy hanging sac.

"Lexi," he pushed her name into her mouth, and it was a sound of desperation that made her blood sing. As if magic suddenly wrapped around them both in a cocoon of physical feelings.

She held his hard length, guiding him to her center, parting herself with his tip. A zing of pleasure shot down her spine and spurred her forward. She sank down on him an inch, but Graeme grabbed her hips, stilling her movements.

"Darlin', I think it'll hurt more this way. You lay on the bed, and I'll—" His words were strained, as if he held himself back. She didn't care for that.

Lexi put her hands over his on her hips and pushed down all the way, seating him deeply and fully inside her. A sharp stab of pain stole all her attention, and she gasped. Her eyes smarted with tears, and she blinked them away.

"Oh, darlin'. Are you okay?"

She forced a nod, but neither of them moved.

"Lexi, do you want to stop?" Graeme's voice was thick and even more strained.

"Am I hurting ye?" she rasped, when his erection jerked inside her.

He chuckled. "Not at all. You feel pretty freaking awesome. I want to move, but I don't want to hurt you."

His arousal jolted inside her again, and this time it shot a tendril of something pleasant down her spine. Lexi shifted her pelvis.

A throb of discomfort answered, but not sharp like when she'd torn through her maidenhead.

Maybe he'd been right, and it would've been gentler if Graeme had controlled how fast they'd come together, but she didn't regret ending her virginity on her own terms. However, she wasn't anywhere near ready for it to be over, either.

Lexi rocked her hips gently to see if the pain returned, and the responding sensation became pleasurable. She did it again, this time with a little more vigor.

Graeme threw his head back on the pillows, much like she had earlier. "Oh, God, Lexi. You're so damn tight." Then his dark eyes went wide. "Wait, wait. We need a condom…"

She didn't understand what a condom was or why he insisted on stopping right then for one. Right when things turned so damn satisfying. She didn't want to ask. She didn't want to wait. She just wanted to keep him inside her and finish what they'd started.

Lexi thrust her hips, undulating harder.

He tightened his grip on her hips, shifting beneath her.

When she thrust again, he guided her movements until they'd found a pleasing rhythm.

She rode him beyond all sense and reasoning,

bracing her palms on his chest. Graeme pulled her down for a kiss, which she deepened, twining their tongues.

He wrapped his arms around her and flipped their bodies, all somehow without pulling out of her. Graeme started to thrust, gently at first, then faster.

Lexi gasped from the shock of body-warmed linens under her shoulders and back, and because his movements inside her felt so different. His clean, masculine scent puffed around her, enveloped her senses, making her feel closer to him.

He plunged forward again, and she whimpered. Unlike the remnants of pain when she'd started moving on top of him, this was all pleasure, shooting all over her form and making her belly warm.

Graeme cupped her bottom and lifted her hips to meet his downward strokes, and she moved with him, under him.

He made her head spin, and she felt the now-familiar sensation of a building orgasm.

She reached for him, grasping his biceps as he drove in and out, hovering over her. Climax crested, and her inner muscles went taut, followed by her limbs and torso, shaking against his muscular body. She screamed her pleasure.

He grunted and groaned her name.

Lexi opened her eyes right as he stilled above her, the cords of his neck prominent and tight, along with the rest of his shoulders and upper body.

He sucked in an audible breath. His cursed softly through closed eyes as his manhood pulsed inside her with a hot gush of his release.

Graeme was beautiful in his passion, his body etched like a finely carved stone statue, his muscles stark and defined, but his face relaxed and unlined. His hair looked like rest of him, attractively mussed, and his face was flushed with color, his lips swollen from their kisses.

He was the most gorgeous man she'd ever seen.

Lexi couldn't breathe for two heartbeats, and her pulse thundered in her ears.

Along with her innocence, she'd also inadvertently given him her heart.

He slid from her body, and lay down beside her, drawing her into his arms, against his chest.

Her mind was a chaos of accusations and questions she was afraid to answer.

"Lexi?" Graeme whispered.

Their gazes met and held.

The smile on his wonderful mouth stalled, and he gripped her shoulders, giving her a gentle shake. "Are you okay?"

Lexi forced a nod, because she couldn't find her voice.

"Lexi." Her name was all warning. "Talk to me. Do you hurt?"

She shook her head and her eyes filled with tears. She bit her bottom lip, because she didn't want to sob like a bairn. Burying her face against his neck kept her from doing something foolish, like blurt out she loved him.

"Oh, Lexi, darlin'. I'm so sorry."

She sucked back a subtle sniffle, and made herself look into his lovely midnight eyes. "Sorry?" she forced out. Hurt threatened to swallow her whole, washing away the pleasant bonelessness in her body.

He didn't regret what they'd done, did he?

"Your first time is supposed to —"

"'Twas perfect," she uttered like a demand.

Graeme offered a small, hesitant smile that made her heart spin into a new chaos. "Yeah?"

"Did I please ye?" Lexi forced out the question she wasn't convinced she really wanted an honest answer to.

"God, you have to ask? I guess I didn't do that great of a job, after all." He cupped her face, his eyes so dark and serious, it stole her breath all over again. "You *always* please me, Lexi-darlin', but tonight blew everything else out of the water. You were more than perfect. You're exquisite." He pressed his lips to her forehead.

"Ye...ye...dinnae regret it, then?"

His brow furrowed and his intense stare was back, boring into her. "Regret it? Hell, no." He dipped down and kissed her.

Lexi snaked her arms around his neck, tried to stave off her tears and kissed him back with all her might. It melted into something languorous, tender and meaningful, and her tummy wobbled from the inside and out.

She'd fallen in love with Graeme MacDonald.

How the hell was she supposed to leave him now?

chapter seventeen

raeme watched her sleep, his heart in his throat. He'd taken her virginity—sans a condom even, then she'd promptly burst into tears. Just the reaction he wanted from the best lover he'd ever had in his life.

No condom?

What the fuck had he been thinking?

Well, he hadn't been *thinking*.

He'd come inside her.

He cursed himself to hell and back.

It wasn't even a worry about STDs. Graeme was clean and normally careful. Couldn't remember the last time he'd had sex without a condom. Maybe when he'd been a dumb teen.

He could've knocked her up tonight.

An unpleasant tremor shot down his spine.

Lexi had amnesia, had no idea about her past, but she *had* been a virgin.

Guilt had threatened to eat him up from the inside out when he'd seen the blood on his dick and smeared on his thighs.

Due to his lack of rational mental thought, Lexi could be memory-less, lost *and* pregnant.

He'd said it, sure, so some part of his brain was

somewhat functional, but she hadn't seemed concerned. Then with one tiny thrust, he was all penis and no sense. Maybe the old saying about God only giving men enough blood to run one "brain" at a time wasn't too far off the mark.

Graeme shoved his hand through his hair. "Fuck."

If — well, more like *when* — who was he kidding? *When* he made love to her again, he would make sure Mr. Happy wore a raincoat.

She'd been so perfect. Exquisite was the best word for it.

He was in so much trouble.

No matter her urgings and declarations that she wanted him, Graeme shouldn't have made love to her, but he didn't regret it.

He couldn't.

Graeme would forever be the first man to touch her, kiss her, take her, as Lexi had so aptly put it before, which had effectively exploded the last of his resistance to nonexistence. That knowledge did funny things to his insides and also made him feel vulnerable. Not very manly of him.

He also couldn't fool himself into believing it was just meaningless sex.

It was so much *more* than that.

Lexi had chosen him to be her first. He was honored. He'd known her for a week, but it felt like years, despite her lack of memory.

A little voice whispered from the back of his mind, and he wanted to ignore it, but he couldn't.

What will you do if she does get pregnant?

Well, he would do right by her, of course.

Graeme blinked.

He would?

Of course, he would, and he'd love every second of it. He cared for her. More than cared for her.

Maybe even loved her?

A vision popped into his mind of Lexi standing in front of the window of his living room of his little cottage, the sun streaming in behind her making her look ethereal, like a haloed angel. She was smiling and caressing a huge round tummy.

That idea should've scared the shit out of him, but it didn't. He'd always assumed he'd do the wife and kids thing one day long down the road.

What if *one day* was sooner?

With the intriguing female he'd found on the beach?

Graeme startled, his stare intent on her peaceful sleeping form.

Lexi was on her side, her long black locks looking mussed and well-loved spread every direction on his pillows. Her eyelashes rested like crescent moons on her high cheekbones, and she was so beautiful it made his breath stall in his chest. The pink flush of passion had faded from her alabaster skin, but his heart tripped anyway.

She was still gloriously naked, and in his bed.

Where she belonged.

Lexi had one hand tucked beneath her chin, and the other was across her body, half-extended, as if she was reaching for him even in her sleep.

Her biceps blocked the view of her perfect breasts,

but Graeme didn't need to see them to remember what they felt like in his hands, his mouth, against his pecs.

She looked so perfect and innocent as she slept, and it made him even more torn.

He couldn't regret what they'd done.

It'd felt right, like no other woman belonged in his arms. It'd been that way from day one, when he'd been compelled to kiss her in the truck on the beach.

She might not know who she was, but *he* did.

Alexandria MacLeod was the woman who'd captured his heart.

In the very short period of a week.

A freaking week.

Graeme loved her.

What the fuck was he supposed to do now?

Her family, whoever they were, could appear any moment, despite the police having no records. Nor she could remember who she was.

If her memory did return, maybe she'd…want to leave him and go home, wherever home was.

Lexi might remember that she had a boyfriend, fiancé, or some shit. Maybe her former life already offered her everything she'd wanted, and decide to go back to it. She'd choose her other life over him.

How the fuck was he supposed to let her go?

His heart slid to his toes.

What if she *wanted* to go?

Even after all they'd shared together.

He was so screwed.

Hell, he'd just invented a whole new way to be jilted.

Graeme had just purchased a one-way ticket to Heartbreakville.

It wasn't like she could just to continue to follow him and Gramps all over Skye—or anywhere else in Scotland the next job took them.

Bridget had told them the day before that a couple who'd purchased a small fifteen-room castle on the Isle of Mull wanted a consultation regarding restoration and remodel, because they had plans to open a bed and breakfast. His grandfather had told her to put it on the books for a few weeks from now. The project at Dunvegan was almost complete.

Graeme swallowed.

His new normal included Lexi, even though it'd only been a week. They even had a routine, from morning, noon and night. She'd fallen into line with Gramps, too, like a natural fit into their team.

Was she the reason his grandfather had softened and started to teach him, like he'd begged the man for the last eight—almost nine months now?

Another reason to keep her around, for sure.

Graeme would have to continue to take things one day at a time, like he'd told Lexi so many times when she'd fretted over memories or half-said statements.

The niggling sense he didn't know the whole truth raised its ugly head again, reminding him there was more to Lexi's story. He rejected it almost instantly, like he always did. It was too painful to consider.

She wasn't a liar.

She hadn't lied about being a virgin.

Lexi had spoken of her mother a few times, her

father once, and then during the driving lesson, a horse. What did it mean?

Could there be more she *wasn't* saying?

His mind circled back to absolute denial, surrounded by why.

Why would she lie?

Was she running from something?

Graeme raked his gaze down her pretty face again, and his heartrate sped up.

This beautiful creature with unusual eyes wasn't a liar.

She was his love.

"Graeme..." she whispered.

He smiled.

She hadn't woken, so the quiet utterance was in her sleep. His fingers ached to touch her again.

He settled beside her on his mattress, pulling her to him. The scent of his soap, shampoo, and the clean detergent on his sheets mixed with a scent that was just Lexi and their lovemaking. It surrounded him and Graeme closed his eyes, breathing in that glorious new fragrance.

Tucking her against him felt natural, normal, like he'd done it all his life.

"Graeme," she muttered his name again, cuddling close to his side, and rested her palm on his abs like she owned him.

The idea had appeal.

"Lexi?" he whispered.

Sleepy violet eyes blinked a few times as she looked up at him, her cheek on his pec. "Hmm."

The sound vibrated against his nipple and it tingled with interest, as did his cock. He smiled and dropped a kiss on her forehead, but she tilted back, inviting him to take her mouth.

Graeme did so, and it was a soft tender thing that made his gut flip over. He loved her, whether she made his body burn with desire or held her like this. There was no rush, no wild climb to orgasm now, just contented pleasure of kissing her, tasting her thoroughly.

"Sorry, I didn't mean to wake you," he said into her lips, and felt her smile against his mouth.

"I dinnae mind o'er much."

He chuckled and kissed her again.

Lexi rubbed her tongue against his, heating things up, until desire thrummed beneath the surface of his skin. He was hard and aching, ready for round two.

Her hands splayed across his pecs, caressing his nipples until they were taut, too. She tickled her fingers through his chest hair, and a bolt of anticipation shot down his spine, landing on his balls. They pulsed like they demanded attention, another release.

"Damn, darlin'," Graeme breathed, tearing his mouth off hers.

"I want ye again," she panted.

He nodded, because it was all he could do. He wouldn't refuse her—he couldn't.

"Hold on a sec." He slipped from his bed and darted over to his dresser.

The drawer where he kept his boxers held some condoms for moments like this, since the bathroom was so far from his bedroom. He ripped one out of the box and clambered back to his bed.

"Do you want to put it on me?" Graeme asked.

Lexi tilted her head to one side, staring at the little foil packet. "What is it?" she whispered.

"A condom. So you don't get pregnant. We should've used one the first time."

An appealing smudge of crimson darkened her already flushed cheeks and she averted her eyes. The dim lights from his nightlights didn't reveal all, but Lexi seemed suddenly leery.

Graeme frowned.

She was embarrassed now?

After all they'd done?

How could she not know what a condom was? She'd been a virgin, sure, but was she that naïve? Maybe her parents had sheltered her, and that was how she'd made it to twenty-one never having had sex with anyone.

"Hey," he whispered, gently guiding her pretty face back to him. "It's okay. If…there are…consequences from our first time, it'll be okay. I'll take care of you."

"Consequences?" Lexi asked in that attractive brogue, her pretty eyes wide.

He nodded. "If you got pregnant." Saying the word was hard, but they were both adults.

They *should* have this conversation.

"I want you again, too. We just need to be responsible this time." Graeme shook the packet.

Lexi's gorgeous breasts heaved, then her shoulders loosened, as if she relaxed. It seemed as if she would say something, but she didn't. She leaned forward and kissed him. "Okay," she whispered into his mouth.

His dick jumped. One little kiss and she'd revved him up again. "Do you want to put it on?" he repeated.

Now she looked shy, but her eyes on his body were like a physical zing. "I dinnae ken..."

"We can do it together."

She nodded, and Graeme ripped the foil open, tossing it over his shoulder when he had the latex in hand.

He guided Lexi's fingers around the condom and, together, they unrolled it down his hard dick. He shivered from her touch, because thin barrier or not, he still wanted her hands everywhere on him.

Graeme lay them down and kissed her again, caressing and nibbling her neck, breasts and collar bone until she writhed beneath him, making the most tempting mewling and whimpering sounds he'd ever heard.

He dragged his fingers down her flat belly and ran two up her sex, circling her clit.

Lexi threw her head back and called his name over and over, like a chant, and he almost lost it.

She was already wet, with barely any foreplay and his cock jumped, his balls aching with the need to take her and come again.

Like he'd never had sex before, let alone sex with her.

He touched her inner thighs, urged her legs wider, then slid inside her with one quick thrust. He groaned and was grateful for the condom, because he might have lost it already if he was skin against skin.

She was so damn tight, and held him like a fitted glove. Her inner muscles clutched at him, trembling against his invasion.

He wanted to thrust, take her hard. He couldn't. This was only her second time, and he needed to be gentle.

Lexi moaned, and grabbed his biceps. "'Tis different. Feels different."

Graeme stilled. "Am I hurting you?"

"Nay, but I prefer yer skin against mine."

He smiled and kissed her quickly. "I know, darlin', me, too. But it has to be this way for now. Maybe we can go to the clinic for birth control."

She didn't respond, so Graeme drove forward, slowly at first, but when Lexi started moving with him, he quickened his pace and followed her lead.

She wrapped her legs around his waist, taking him deeper, and he was quickly lost in her.

In her arms, with her touches, kisses…

There was only Lexi.

He loved her. Wanted to tell her, but it was so unfair to her.

She'd eventually leave him to return to her life. He couldn't put the pressure of romantic feelings on her or demand that she choose to stay with him.

Graeme crushed his eyes shut, concentrating on their bodies moving together, brushing and rubbing. Each plummet forward took him higher. Every time she called his name, it made him soar, too.

His spine tingled; his balls jumped.

He was close.

Lexi cried out, and her nails dug into his arms, but he didn't give a shit if she made him bleed. Her sex contracted, gripping his cock hard, then the waves of her inner muscles tightening and relaxing tossed him over the edge of her orgasm.

He came hard, grunted forward with one last thrust with enough force to make his bed creak. Everything surged down to the singular point of release, stealing all ability to pump his blood throughout the rest of his body. His chest heaved and he panted, because lack of oxygen made him lightheaded.

Graeme rolled to his back so he wouldn't crush her, but Lexi wasn't having it.

She threw her leg over his middle and dragged his mouth to hers. When she shoved her tongue against his lips, he let her in, reveled in her clutching his neck almost too-tight and kissing him until the weightless, airless sensation was back, dancing behind his eyes.

If he died like this, it would be okay. He would've lived his best life.

He broke their lip-lock only because his lungs demanded oxygen, but he held her forehead to his.

I love you was on the tip of his tongue, but he banished it and really looked at her, pink cheeks, mussed hair, purple eyes.

She was ravished. Graeme's heart took off all over again.

Lexi smiled, and it was somehow sated, with a side of shyness. Her appealing sense of innocence was there, even without the V-Card. Something else was there, too. Vixen, and it was an intriguing mix.

She was the most beautiful woman he'd ever seen and Graeme had no idea how he could hold onto her.

Fine time to finally fall in love.

His heart slid to his gut and ached, chasing away some of his post-coital bliss.

"Somethin' wrong?" Lexi whispered.

"Oh, no, darlin'. How could something be wrong? Are you okay? You're not in pain?"

She smiled again. "Nay. Ye make me feel good, like always."

"You make me feel good, too." Although, *good* was the understatement of the century. He slipped from the bed, pinching the condom and sliding it off, so he could dispose of it. "Be right back, darlin'. I'll bring a washcloth to clean you up, like last time."

Graeme dashed to the bathroom like someone was on his ass, because he didn't want to be away from her one second longer than necessary.

He ditched the rubber, cleaned up, and stared at himself in the mirror above the sink. He gripped the sides of the porcelain with both hands, his gaze boring into his reflection.

"What the fuck are you doing?" he demanded in a harsh whisper.

I don't know was the silent answer.

He shoved his hand through his hair on a sigh, cursed and grabbed a light purple washcloth from the rack on the wall next to the mirror. It wouldn't have been his color choice, but like the furniture and appliances, the cottage came fully stocked on linens and towels, too.

Graeme let the water run until it was almost too-hot,

and hissed when he rang out the terrycloth. When he closed his eyes, all he could see were Lexi's, staring up at him like he'd hung the moon.

His heart skipped, and he hurried back to his room.

He couldn't tell he loved her, but he sure as hell could hold onto her for as long as she'd let him.

chapter eighteen

exi showered alone, but it was fine, because she needed to gather her thoughts. She didn't know what to say to Graeme, and that was an odd feeling.

She'd never been at a loss for words with her American MacDonald—except when she'd been trying to play off a slip of the tongue regarding her supposedly lost memories.

Her body ached pleasantly in all the right places, and she had no regrets about the two times she'd given herself to him completely.

The water sluiced over her naked body and she inhaled the scent of his soap and what he'd called shampoo, as it was all around her in the humid warm air.

Graeme had offered to buy Lexi her own—more feminine soap and shampoo, he'd said—but she'd refused. She liked smelling like him, using his supplies.

Every time he'd smiled at her in the hours that'd past since she'd given him her innocence, all she wanted to do was shout that she loved him. Yet, she couldn't tell him that truth, nor any of her other truths.

Lexi had to return to her family, even though she didn't want to. Leaving Graeme with words of love would only make for a more difficult parting.

She needed to go.

Soon.

How?

She couldn't just disappear on him.

He cared for her, as he'd said, although those were not words of love, either. He would worry if she went without warning.

She couldn't tell him the truth before she fled, either.

Could she leave him a written note?

Would his grandfather tell him of her admission he'd surely never believe, once she was gone?

Lexi crushed her eyes against tears she didn't want to deal with, and put her face in the hot spray of water. She ran her hands over her heavy wet locks, and rubbed her body down with his bar of soap, washing her arms and legs.

She rinsed off and cleaned her breasts, then smoothed her palm down her stomach. She paused above her sex, recalling what Graeme had said about pregnancy.

When she'd formulated her mission to give herself to him, she hadn't contemplated a child, although her mother had told her how new life was created.

What she'd experienced with Graeme had been beautiful, and if their first coupling resulted in a child, Lexi would be more than fine with that. She would have a piece of him to hold forever.

Her heart quickened.

Foolish lass.

Graeme had been right to use what he'd called protection the second time they'd made love. He'd still taken her to soaring heights, but she didn't like such a barrier between them from the material of the condom.

She wanted him always as she'd had him the first time, with nothing inhibiting their complete connection except skin. She'd felt him completely, experienced him *completely*.

Lexi should be praying there was no child, because having a child with a man born over three hundred years after she, a man whom she was not married to, was the worst idea...ever.

If her belly rounded once she'd returned home, her father and uncles would no doubt march to the future, claymores drawn. Hopefully, her mother would refuse to open the Faery Stones.

Her pulse stuttered again. She wouldn't let any harm come to the man she loved, and if she did carry his child, maybe her family would give their blessing to stay with him?

Would Graeme MacDonald want what *she* wanted, once he knew the truth of how she'd come to be in his time?

Three women in her family had come to her time, married and stayed, more than three centuries from when they belonged.

Could that be her fate, too?

Only in the reverse. She'd seen the wonders of what her Aunt Claire had called "modern days," and wanted to see more, learn more.

Graeme said he would take care of her if there was a child. He'd also told her she could stay with him as long as she wanted.

Was *forever* an option?

A new round of tears pressed behind her eyes, and Lexi wiped her face, then returned to the warm cascade of water.

It all seemed so impossible.

She wanted to fix things with her mother.

She wanted to stay with Graeme.

One would only be possible at the cost of the other.

"Lexi, breakfast is ready."

Lexi screeched and scrambled to grab the metal bar on the shower wall.

"Oh, Jesus!" Graeme whipped the glass shower door open and grabbed for her. "I'm so sorry, I didn't mean to startle you." He plastered her to his chest.

She looked into his wide, dark eyes and laughed. Her fright immediately gone with the phrase that reminded her so much of home, something her father, Uncle Duncan, and even her brother said often.

His brows were tight, confused. "Are you all right?" he demanded.

She nodded and smiled. "I'm gettin' ye all wet."

The shower water still ran, soaking the back of his shirt, as her body did the same to the front. His heart pattered against her breasts, revealing his fear of her almost-fall, but her love laughed, something she felt as well as heard. "I would prefer to be the one getting *you* wet."

Lexi giggled, threw her arms around his neck and kissed him.

When Graeme joined her in the kitchen, Lexi sat on her usual stool at the counter, kicking her feet like a little kid and eating a slice of toast.

The scent of fresh coffee wafted through the room, and a mug steamed next to her small plate.

He was mesmerized by the movement of her bare, very shapely, very adult legs.

Graeme grinned and ran the towel over his damp hair. Her scare in the shower had quickly flipped into him stripping out of his clothing and joining her, where he proceeded to take her again, against the tile wall, using that safety handrail for delicious leverage. Evidently, he couldn't keep his hands to himself where Lexi MacLeod was concerned.

Again, they hadn't used a condom, but instead of coming inside her, he'd pulled out. He called himself every name in the book afterwards, because the pull-out method wasn't anywhere near one hundred percent effective. He needed to litter condoms all over the cottage so he wouldn't have any excuses.

Since when had he been an irresponsible idiot when it came to sex?

Since Lexi.

He loved her, which made it so much more difficult. Making love was worse than a woman leading him around by his dick for sex, because his heart was much more complicated than mere hormones.

"Mornin'," Lexi said over the rim of her mug, as if

she hadn't just rocked his world mere minutes before.

She wore one of his shirts, instead of one from her array purchased from Flora's shop. The black fabric hung loose, revealing a cream, delectable shoulder. He couldn't see what she had on the bottom, so it was either shorts or just panties, and wasn't that an awesome picture?

Graeme went to her, pulled the shirt upright, covering her bare skin, and kissed her still-damp head. He inhaled and closed his eyes, loving his scent all over her. "Mornin', darlin'."

"I made ye toast." She grinned triumphantly, as if she'd won the lottery or something, and he chuckled.

"I like toast, thank you."

Lexi always appeared inordinately pleased with herself when she accomplished any task, no matter how minor or small, and it was just one more thing he loved about her. It was as adorable as she was.

The scrambled eggs and bacon he'd made prior to their shower had long gone cold. He offered to warm the already-plated food in the microwave, and took a bite of the toast. She'd buttered it, and the appealing salty flavor rolled over his tongue.

"I can do it," she said, sliding off the stool. She pushed the microwave door's release button.

Lexi concentrated so hard, like she'd done when he'd taught her to drive, and all he could do was smile as he watched.

She pressed the *1* button and the sixty second countdown started.

When the machine *dinged*, his love threw him

another grin over her again-bare shoulder.

Graeme chuckled. How she always managed to be an enticing, innocent vixen, he could never guess, but he wasn't going to complain, either. She was just perfect.

He loved her so damn much.

His stomach dipped, threatening to eject the bread he'd just eaten, but he blew out a breath and joined Lexi by the microwave. "Thanks, darlin'," he whispered, but he really meant, *I love you.*

She warmed up the other plate of food and they ate at the counter, sitting across from each other. Probably a good thing to have distance between them for a time. Graeme really needed to keep his hands to himself.

"What do you want to do today?"

"We dinnae go ta Dunvegan?"

He shook his head. "No, it's Sunday. Back to work tomorrow, though, bright and early."

Lexi's expression was thoughtful, but she didn't remark.

He could take her over to Mallaig on the ferry. The little village was cute, and there were a lot of shops and touristy places. "Do you like ice cream?"

"Ice cream?" she repeated the two words, as if she'd never said them before.

Did she really have no idea what ice cream was?

Graeme told himself to let that go and nodded. "Yes. You know, chocolate, vanilla, creamy cold deliciousness?"

She smirked.

He wanted to lick into that corner of her mouth. Awareness zinged down his spine, mixed with tempting memories.

Oh yeah, he needed to get her out of his cottage for the day, or he would just hold her hostage in his bed. Not that she'd complain.

Graeme cleared his throat and sat taller. Ordered his dick to calm down. "We can take the ferry to Mallaig for the day. There are shops, places to eat, museums, even a bookstore. But my favorite place is this little café with homemade ice cream."

Lexi smiled, but still didn't speak.

"We can pretend we're tourists."

"Okay," she finally said.

"Good, should be fun."

Lexi took a sip of coffee and set down her mug.

"Well, darlin' as much as I adore looking at you nearly naked, you'll have to get dressed."

She flashed a grin, shot him a visual dare, and slid off the stool.

Graeme ordered himself to stay where he was, or they wouldn't make it to Mallaig after all.

chapter nineteen

Lexi was convinced they were going to drown.

Graeme drove the truck right *onto* what he'd called a ferry, and Lexi had to suck back a gasp. He'd told her they didn't have to stay inside the vehicle, so he took her to seats on the top level of the floating marvel.

This was unlike any boat she'd ever boarded in her life.

They went all the way up to the highest deck, and Lexi looked down to see the blue truck in a line of other cars and trucks also leaving Skye for Mallaig. People mingled about the decks, some sitting and some standing, or walking the decks. She did neither. Instead, she peered over the edge, white knuckles gripping the side railing and studying their surroundings. How in the world did this boat keep everyone and all the cars afloat?

The blue waters, tiny isles, and distant mountains inched past them, the wind in her hair. Lexi closed her eyes as it caressed her cheeks and shot a chill down her spine.

Her hair tickled her cheeks and neck, and she shivered in what Graeme had called a hoodie. It was light purple, and had a zipper and pockets she loved. The hood was like a proper mantle, but she didn't have it on her head.

It wasn't a cold day, but the wind was vigorous on the ferry's top deck.

She felt his eyes on her, and met his beautiful dark gaze.

"Somethin' wrong?" she asked, smiling.

He crowded her against the railing, but she reveled in his body heat and closeness. He was so much bigger than her, and never failed to make her feel safe.

"Not at all." Graeme nuzzled the side of her neck and pulled her shoulders into his chest, wrapping his strong arms around her. "You're just so damn gorgeous."

She smiled and snuggled into him, resting her head on him and letting him hold her. Her heart skipped and she tremored from the tease of his warm breath on the skin below her ear.

"So are ye," Lexi whispered. She loved this man so much, her American MacDonald from the future.

He chuckled, the sound rumbling against her.

Graeme held her for the duration of the thirty-minute boat ride, then they went back down to the truck to debark.

He'd called his grandfather and told him where they would be for the day, and asked if the man needed anything.

Gramps asked them to pick up and order from a local craftsman, and Graeme agreed. They added a stop at a small specialty woodworking shop, he'd called it.

James asked to speak with her. The younger man at her side looked surprised, but Lexi put the phone to her ear.

The older man spoke in Gaelic, likely because he didn't want to be overheard by his grandson. If Graeme heard the other language, he wouldn't understand it anyway.

"Be careful," was the admonition in her ear.

Lexi wasn't sure what to say, so she listened.

James went on to tell her she would see things like she never had before, and that he wasn't warning her to scare her, but to be mindful of what she said to Graeme.

She answered in the affirmative and smiled when the man told her he would see her the next day.

"What was that about?" Graeme asked.

"He tol' me ta have a good time," Lexi stumbled through the lie and tried to ignore the answering guilt.

Her lover frowned, but accepted his phone and pocketed it. He didn't say anything else, so she slipped her hand into his.

When Graeme had told her about Mallaig, aside from the ferry and something called ice cream, what was before her now revealed she'd understood even less than she imagined. The village hadn't been there in her time, yet another thing she couldn't admit or even comment on.

Hiding her lies was getting harder, especially when he introduced her to things she'd never heard of. Even new towns and trying to make connections to her own time. He always studied her a bit too hard when Lexi struggled for an appropriate response. In those moments, he was like Gramps, as if he looked right through her. Had to be a MacDonald trait.

They parked in the harbor parking lot, alongside

many others who'd left the ferry with them.

Lexi didn't know where to look first. The sights around her were so amazing, she kept hollering at herself to maintain a placid countenance, but it was so hard to hide her wonder.

Mallaig was supposed to be a small village, according to Graeme, but to her it was big and appealing, the place made her recall when her family had visited Edinburgh some years past.

People milled about everywhere, families, couples and children all talking, laughing, walking in and out of shops, or eating at cafés, he'd called them. Cars drove up and down the narrow streets, but most people seemed to be on foot, like them.

His grandfather had been right to warn her. She couldn't say anything that would clue Graeme in on her being out of touch with the time.

That she'd been lying.

The nice, warm spring day made her wanted to run up and down the pathways, take it all in as she gasped and pointed, and show how truly awesome she found it all, but she couldn't chance the questions that would create.

"C'mon, let's get some ice cream," Graeme said, tucking her arm into his. "Then we'll pick up that stuff for Gramps."

Graeme didn't want to sit inside the crowded little shop on such a nice day, so he asked Lexi to sit on the bench on the sidewalk across from the entrance, so no one else could claim it.

Despite the disappointed expression she gave him, he'd kissed the frown off her face and promised to bring her a chocolate cone, as she'd requested.

He couldn't stop watching her.

Lexi observed and studied Mallaig in mostly silence, but her gorgeous wide eyes looked at everything as if she'd never seen it before, just like when they'd driven onto the ferry.

The isle of Skye was remote, for sure, but it was still somewhat modern.

Sometimes Lexi said something that felt so old-school, it made him wonder. Just how sheltered had her parents kept her, wherever she'd grown up on the isle. Cloistered somewhere?

Did she come from some religious cult?

One that allowed their women to swim naked in the Minch?

Graeme snorted.

He wanted to ask so many questions he didn't think she'd answer, and he didn't want to imply he thought she was lying, even if the little doubt monster in the back of his head wouldn't shut the hell up.

The woman he'd fallen in love with wasn't a liar.

He shook his head and threw a glance over his shoulder to make sure she was okay on the bench as he waited in line to order.

Lexi was so damn pretty, her hair loose and shifting in the breeze, one leg crossed over the other in her jeans. Her lilac hoodie was zipped all the way up, but he was okay with her boobs not being on display.

She seemed to be openly people watching, staring as they came and went along the sidewalk.

The guy behind the counter finally called on him to take their order. Graeme couldn't get back to Lexi fast enough.

Her eyes went wide all over again with the first lick of the chocolate cone. "Hmm…" she said, licking her lips, then diving in for another taste.

He chuckled. His mind drifted to all the other places her tongue had been just that morning. The thought made his dick rise to attention.

Stop it.

He needed a distraction to avoid tight jeans in an inappropriate setting. Graeme leaned in, and put a dot of vanilla ice cream on her nose.

Lexi gave a shriek of surprise, and crossed her eyes, trying to focus on it.

She was so damn adorable.

Graeme chuckled. "Sorry," he said, but he wasn't sorry in the least.

When her violet gaze landed on his, she giggled. "Ye dinnae seem it!" she exclaimed, but her playful expression shouted she was far from mad.

"C'mere."

They met halfway and he dropped a kiss on her nose, sucking off the ice cream.

Lexi tilted up her mouth, and pressed her lips to his.

Graeme pushed his tongue inside, tasting the chocolate remnants, but told himself not to get lost in her kiss. They were on a bench in public, and on the nice sunny warm Sunday afternoon in a tourist spot; there were tons of people around. Not that he cared about having an audience, but it wasn't like he could strip her naked and take her right on the pavement.

He broke the kiss when some giggling penetrated his sex-fogged brain. He pulled away gently, but had to suck back a groan when he looked at his lover's face.

She was already flushed deliciously pink up to her ears, and her purple eyes were heavy-lidded.

Damn, he wanted her.

Three teenage girls across the street openly stared, laughed and whispered. They also had ice cream cones in hand, and must've just come out of the shop.

Lexi flashed a smile for him, as if she didn't notice the girls—or didn't care. "Ye were right," she announced.

"About?" Graeme settled back against the bench, and slid his arm around her shoulders. He wrapped the napkin higher on his cone to catch the melting parts. One thought about how to clean off sticky fingers had his mind—and his cock—right back where it shouldn't be in his current sitch.

"Ice cream…'tis good!" She licked her chocolate cone.

He smiled and nodded, then made himself eat the vanilla ice cream, because if he didn't, he would kiss her again, or explore if any of the hotels in Mallaig had rooms to rent by the hour.

chapter twenty

The next few days passed in a blink. Graeme was so lost in Lexi and their constant sex; it was hard to focus on anything outside of that safe little bubble of them alone in his cottage.

It was more than that, though. They were living together, working together, and all those moments between together as well. A period of his life he'd always cherish, and might come to an end at any moment.

He loved her and couldn't imagine her going.

Didn't want to think about the day she'd wake with her memories restored.

Lexi would contact her family and leave him.

Not even a job he enjoyed would help him survive the loss.

He and Gramps were closing in on finishing the double hearth project at Dunvegan Castle—perhaps a day or two left, then they would check out the potential project on Mull.

Bridget had confirmed Mr. and Mrs. Cheney for a consultation on the following Monday. Turned out they were also Americans, from Iowa, and had already been working on their new home for a few months, but they wanted to bring out some of the historical features.

He was excited at the prospect of starting a new

project. Determining how far back in history they'd travel, the resources they'd source, and how big of a crew they'd need. Normally, his grandfather had a regular group of guys he worked with, but the hearths at Dunvegan hadn't required them.

Graeme hauled the canvas bag from the back of the truck. He'd already brought the restored wood he'd picked up from Mallaig into the great hall.

His phone *binged* with a reminder, and he put the bag down to dig it from his pocket. His sense of dread assaulted him when the appointment popped up on his calendar.

Lexi, Doc Guinn for MRI

This was the happy little twenty-four hours out reminder. The visit was at ten the next morning.

He didn't want to take her. Didn't want them to find a valid reason for her memory loss, like a brain tumor or something. Besides, she'd been so scared at the clinic two weeks ago. Weeks that felt like months, for sure, or even years, but it didn't change the fact Graeme couldn't take that petrified look on her face again.

MRIs were so nerve-wracking. He'd had one on his knee in college because of a football injury, and though he wasn't claustrophobic or anything, he'd wanted to run from the thumping noises and overbearing machinery as soon as it was finished. It was like having a big rig engine right in his ears.

He didn't want to put his sweet Lexi through that experience.

Or maybe he didn't want to encourage her memory to return, so she could stay with him forever.

Graeme cursed himself and shoved his phone back in his pocket. When he looked up, his gaze landed on the woman he loved, striding toward him.

She wore a tight gray T-shirt with the words, "Mallaig, established 1840" screen-printed across the chest, along with an image made to look like an old stamp of a boat across her breasts.

He'd bought it on their day trip, the fabric fitted to her form as if it made for her. He couldn't look away.

"Yer grandfa sent me ta see what's takin' ye so long," Lexi said, but she smiled, as if to soften the old man's demand.

Meaning, *don't kill the messenger.*

Graeme shook his head, but he wasn't really irritated. "I'm coming, I'm coming," he groused.

She pushed to her tiptoes and pressed a kiss to his cheek. "Dinnae be cross wit' Gramps."

He cocked his head to the side. "Oh, I see where your loyalties lie."

Lexi laughed. "With ye both, a'course."

Graeme grinned. "Good, darlin', I'm glad." He wanted to tell her he loved her, but he bit the words back for the thousandth time.

They went into the castle, Lexi's hips swaying in front of him, and he didn't mind that at all. He watched how her ass moved in tight denim and thanked Flora again for jeans that looked painted on.

They rounded the corner into the great hall, laughing and talking.

He paused; it was too quiet. No sound of a tool moving against wood, or even the radio to which

Gramps usually listened as he worked.

Lexi cried out, then suddenly dashed across the large space.

Graeme followed her gaze. "Gramps," he breathed. Panic clawed its way from his gut straight up to his heart.

His grandfather was lying unmoving in front of the double hearths in the great hall of Dunvegan Castle.

The small stepladder lay on its side, and he did the math quickly.

He dropped the canvas bag and rushed to Gramps' side.

Lexi was already on her knees on his grandfather's other side by the time he slid to the stone floor.

"Gramps," Graeme demanded, but there wasn't a response. He scanned the older man from head to foot. There was no visible blood, so he hadn't hit his head, and even if he'd been on the top step of the three-step folding ladder, the fall wasn't more than four or five feet.

Had his hip gone out?

He shook his grandfather's shoulder. "Lexi, call 9-9-9. He tossed his phone to her. Tell them where we are. He's seventy-two and had a hip replacement six months ago."

Her violet eyes widened, but he watched her press the three numbers with her index finger, ensuring she had it before he looked back at Gramps.

Soon she was talking to a dispatcher, and stumbling her way through answers.

"Gramps," he said again. He'd been CPR certified at one time, but it'd been years. He wracked his brain for those memories.

Graeme leaned over and put his ear to his grandfather's mouth. Thank God the man was breathing on his own.

He tuned out Lexi's tremulous voice and put his knuckles to the older man's chest, rubbing his sternum, praying he could rouse him.

Finally, after what seemed forever, James MacDonald blinked open his dark brown eyes.

"Gramps! What happened? Where do your hurt?" Graeme demanded.

Lexi was back at his side, his phone in her hand. "They said ten minutes." The worry in her purple eyes made his heart ache and his stomach jump.

"Dinnae fash o'er me," Gramps ordered, trying to sit up.

Graeme put his hand on the man's chest, holding him in place. "Stay there, paramedics are coming."

"Nay," the old man said.

"Aye," he said, hard. "It's already done. Tell me where you hurt. Your hip? And don't lie to me."

His grandfather looked away from him, to Lexi.

She offered a wobbly smile and took his hand.

When Gramps spoke, he still looked at her. "My…chest…hurts."

"Your chest?" Alarm washed over Graeme. "Did you fall off the ladder?"

Gramps nodded and closed his eyes.

It scared the shit out of him.

All the blood drained from his head and he was dizzy. A pain in the chest meant a possible cardiac issue, a pulmonary embolism, a thousand other medical issues of which all were extremely bad. Something Graeme couldn't fix.

No, he couldn't lose Gramps right now. There was still far too much left to learn, to resolve between them. The man still had a lot left in him, and he just couldn't leave now.

He screamed at himself to get it together and grabbed his grandfather's shoulders, shaking him hard. "Gramps!"

His grandfather glared. "Stop shakin' me abou'."

Graeme cursed and blew out a breath. "Don't go to sleep. Talk to us."

Gramps looked at Lexi, reaching for her.

His love scooted closer, and leaned over the older man, her eyes misty.

Shock rolled over Graeme when his grandfather lifted a shaky hand and caressed Lexi's cheek.

She cradled his hand in hers.

They started speaking Gaelic, his grandfather's words breathy and spaced, like he struggled for air.

Please, stay with me. Don't leave now.

Graeme followed the ambulance to the clinic like a madman.

Lexi stayed with Gramps in the back of the ambo, since the man refused to let go of her hand. Probably a good thing, since Graeme was just a bag of panic and nerves that she clearly wouldn't find appealing.

The paramedics hadn't said much when they'd

stabilized the older man enough to move, but he wasn't an idiot. He'd caught words like possible coronary, myocardial infarction and even congenital defect.

Those were heart words.

To him, these were all different ways to say the same horrifying thing, a heart attack.

Graeme swallowed against the sudden lump in his throat. His blinked back the tears blurring his vision, because he was driving and he didn't need to do something stupid, like rear-end the ambulance and make things even worse.

They finally reached the clinic, and he slammed the truck into park and was out before the back doors of the ambulance were open.

Lexi jumped down into his arms and he shifted them both out of the way so the two medics could lower the gurney.

"Graeme," she whispered.

"It'll be okay," he said, for her benefit as much as his own.

It *had* to be okay.

He refused to lose the only family he had left.

Doctor Guinn and three other people in scrubs met the paramedics and quickly maneuvered Gramps into a room, where they'd tune everything out, and swarmed the older man, hooking him up to wires and machines.

Graeme took a step into the room, Lexi in tow. Their fingers entwined, he pinned her to his side. She looked terrified, wide-eyed and mouth agape.

"Please, wait outside, Mr. MacDonald, Ms. MacLeod," one of the nurses said, while she hung a bag of clear liquid, probably saline, on the metal holder next to the bed.

She was the one he'd referred to as Scottish Nurse Ratchet the day he'd come in with Lexi two weeks ago.

He rammed his free hand through his hair and nodded. He wanted to be at his grandfather's bedside, but he wanted them to fix him first. He and Lexi would only be in the way.

Graeme led her to the small waiting area at the front.

They slid into chairs, and the receptionist behind the desk cast them looks of sympathy.

The girl couldn't be much older than Lexi, and her carrot-orange hair was pulled into a high ponytail, making her look even younger. She read a magazine, instead of working on the computer in front of her.

They waited.

Waited some more.

Minutes felt like hours, and the analog clock on the wall made a *clicking* noise every time the hands moved.

That made it feel worse somehow. Like counting down the minutes left in Gramp's life. Each agonizing second after another.

They didn't speak, but Lexi was as close to him as possible, and when she leaned into his side, he slid his arm around her shoulders. Their hands remained intwined.

Her touch helped keep him calm.

The phone at the front desk rang.

Graeme jumped.

The call was short, and although they weren't that far from the counter, he didn't hear the exchange.

"Mr. MacDonald?" the girl asked.

"Yes." He stood, rubbing his hands on his thighs.

"Doc Guinn said you can see him now."

"Oh, thank God," he breathed, tears pricking his eyes.

Forcing the emotions back, he hurried back down the small hallway, Lexi on his heels.

They made it his grandfather's bedside, where Scottish Nurse Ratchet adjusted the IV and pulled the blue blanket a little higher on Gramps' chest.

The older man wore a hospital johnny. How in the world had managed to get him in that thing? Maybe because he'd been unconscious.

"Gramps, how you feeling?" he asked.

The man was awake and glaring. "They been pokin' an' proddin' me, how do ye think I'm feelin'?"

Graeme almost smiled.

"Just rest, Mr. MacDonald," the nurse said with a pat to his hand, before she slipped from the room.

Lexi touched his grandfather's arm and the older man locked eyes with her. She said something in Gaelic, and he answered quietly, his face relaxing a little.

Yeah, she has that effect on me, too.

"Mr. MacDonald?" Dr. Guinn spoke.

Graeme almost jumped again, because he hadn't heard the man's approach.

"Dr. Guinn. How is he?" he asked.

"Let's have a word in the hallway." He gestured for Graeme and Lexi to follow out of the room.

Graeme's heart slid to his guts.

The man's expression was so stoic, but his

demeanor was sad, regretful.

This wouldn't be good.

"Your grandfather had a heart attack, as suspected."

"How do we fix it? He'll get better, right?"

Dr. Guinn shook his head, his brown eyes compassionate, yet resolved. "I'm sorry, Mr. MacDonald. The damage is significant."

"No." The denial was hard and fast and he scanned his grandfather's not-so-small form in the bed over the English doctor's shoulder.

Somehow, Gramps looked so weak and boneless, despite his height and large frame.

Graeme's body, his heart — maybe his soul — denied what his eyes and the slow unsteady beep of the heart monitor were trying to tell him. "He was fine *yesterday*."

"Aye, but he wasn't. Not really. With damage this extensive, I suspect the heart failure has been present for a while." The doctor's voice was low and even, as if he was trying to calm Graeme, despite the bad news.

Was that supposed to make him feel better?

"Heart failure?" he whispered.

The doctor nodded. "Perhaps it was the cause of the fall that shattered his hip. I'm only sorry we didn't catch it then."

Graeme glared. "What?"

Lexi tugged on his arm.

He was able to take a fortifying breath, and threw her a glance of thanks. Then he met the doctor's dark eyes. "So, what are the next steps?"

Dr. Guinn maintained his gaze, but his expression was stamped with regret. "There's not much we can do,

Mr. MacDonald, as I was trying to explain."

"I can't accept that."

"Mr. MacDonald—"

"No, Dr. Guinn, you don't understand. I just got him back. I can't lose him. I just *can't*. Don't give me the crap that he's too old, just tell him how you're gonna fix him. If we have to go to the mainland hospital, I'll take him, or get a helicopter, or whatever. Just save my grandfather." It was a rude order, but he didn't care.

They'd just gained some ground; he couldn't lose the man now.

Lexi slid in front of him, and the doctor moved back to give her room.

Graeme startled. Hadn't realized that with every word of his little rant, he'd moved closer, and he was practically in the man's face. He should apologize to the doctor, who was only doing his job, but the words wouldn't be born.

His love filled his line of sight, and cupped his face, forcing him to look in her eyes.

Any other time, he would've slipped into those fathomless violet eyes, but he caught Lexi's urgency, as well as the desire to distract him from more shouting in the doctor's face.

"Graeme. Graeme." She said his name like a chant, and he couldn't look away. Her eyes went misty, and she swallowed, as if she needed a breath of strength, too.

"Lexi—"

Her whisper stopped him. "I can save Gramps."

chapter twenty-one

l exi slammed the shifter into park and shut the truck off like Graeme had shown her. She hadn't exactly asked his permission to take the vehicle, but she couldn't get to the beach any faster.

She wasn't calm enough to *blink* and it could be dangerous if she didn't have a clear picture of her destination in her head. She hadn't tried to do it since coming to the future, so she was also unsure if her magic would answer her call with enough strength to do so.

Sheer panic had threatened to take her over when he'd thrown his cellphone to her and ordered her to call 9-9-9. She hadn't known why, or how to handle what he asked of her, but she'd done it.

Lexi had managed to speak to the woman who'd answered, and told them they were at Dunvegan Castle. She'd answered the woman's questions about James, and she'd even managed his age, since Graeme had told her Gramps was two and seventy.

She was still shaking all over, so not trying to *blink* was the right decision. The terrain resembled what it looked like in her time, but when someone traveled with the power of magic and the mind, the vision of where they wished to go had to be exact.

Lexi also hadn't been back to the beach since the day

Graeme had found her, so she couldn't chance it, in case her memory about what she'd seen was off. Traveling through centuries had made her mind hazy then.

She slammed the truck's door, but left the keys inside, so at least he could retrieve them if he wanted to. She scrambled down the embankment and ran down the beach until she spotted the opening of the cave of the Faery Stones.

The space looked different than before. She pushed her way through the narrow entrance, her magic tingling down her spine, and little rocks and stones tumbling against her body as she displaced them.

Her mother's spell vibrated against her mind. Even after several hundred years, the powerful magic was still in place. No doubt it was the reason the cave had been left untouched, and the Stones still protected. For humans, it was supposed to act as a deterrent, make them feel a sense of dread or repulsion to avoid the area.

Lexi would have to tell her it was still there when she got home.

She shed her clothes and left them in a messy pile on the cave's loamy floor. That way, she'd at least have something to wear when she returned.

Lexi rushed to the Faery Stones, and her fingers were frantic as she woke the main Stone and followed the required pattern.

Magic floated over her form, thrumming from her insides out. The energy felt so familiar and welcoming, she had to close her eyes to take it all in.

What the hell was she doing?

She should *never* have promised Graeme she could

save James MacDonald, with all the rules about not using magic in front of others, the risk that caused, the damage that could unfold.

Lexi had to try.

Her mother had healing powers, as did her Uncle Xander, a former Fae Warrior.

They would help, wouldn't they?

Doubt crept in from the corners of her mind. When Lila, her sister-by-marriage had arrived in their time, her da had taken a tumble from his young stallion and had broken his leg badly. The bone had been sticking out, and her mother hadn't been able to heal him. Lila, the surgeon from the future, was forced to operate to save his life.

Could her mother's magic help Gramps?

I have to try.

There wasn't much magic in the future, but *she* had magic, too. She could feel it in Graeme's time, even if faint. Even if it took all her energy.

Her mother wouldn't deny her, would she?

Lexi's words had hurt her badly, and she'd heard nothing from any of her meddling family in the week that had passed from the confrontation in the gardens.

A shudder shot down her spine.

Her blood wouldn't turn her away…would they?

She put the fears out of her mind and concentrated on the Faery Stones and opening the portal. She'd arrive back in 1694 naked, but she'd run all the way to Dunvegan without a stitch if she had to.

Lexi needed her mother.

She had to save Graeme's grandfather.

A man she'd come to adore, as much as her lover.

James MacDonald hadn't rejected her when she'd revealed she was half Fae, and from the distant past. Hadn't even questioned her much. He'd considered her a member of his family from that moment, and protected her from Graeme's questions she wasn't ready to answer.

She hadn't told her love how she planned to save the older man, but he'd agreed to trust her. That was good, in the least. How she'd explain the rest would have to be for later, when her mother, and perhaps her Uncle Xander were at James' bedside.

How would Graeme take the news that she was from over three hundred years in the past, and that she was only half human?

Or that she intended to save his grandfather with magic — something in which he surely had no faith?

Would he set her aside, even though they'd made love so many times she'd lost count?

Even though she loved him?

No matter that she hadn't told him.

Neither had Graeme talked of feelings, of course. Other than desire and need of her.

The portal took longer than it should to open, likely because she was so fraught with doubt. Lexi cursed her high emotional distraction. She glided her fingers over the Stones again, repeating the pattern and crushed her eyes shut, throwing her mind into the melody and the magic.

She had to put forth mor effort than when she'd left 1694 and she banished the sudden panic that the Faery

Stones just might not work anymore.

Lexi could feel the magic, even if sluggish, so it couldn't be true.

Her heart hammered in her temples, reverberated in her ears, and she shivered, but not because she was naked in the chilly cave.

She forced two more breaths and wiggled her toes in the stark white sand that littered the floor. She slammed her palm down on the middle Stone and prayed.

Relief washed over her as the warm magical gale caressed her bare skin. The first *pop* echoed in the air, followed by three more, and the sound of ripping parchment.

"Thank God," she whispered and her eyes smarted with tears. She blinked them back. She couldn't cry now, she had to go home.

Lexi fell through the portal.

"Lexi."

Her name in a familiar brogue made her blink. She squinted up into an equally familiar pair of sapphire eyes.

"Angus!" Lexi popped to her feet, then listed to one side, her whole body wobbling and her knees threatening to fail.

"Easy, lass." Her brother snatched her arm; the only thing that kept the silty terrain outside the cave from reaching up and grabbing her.

She must've been lying on the ground again. She sucked in air to clear her head, but it was still spinning.

"Time travel's, a bitch, huh?" Humor darted across her sister-by-marriage's pretty face.

Her brother smirked.

"Here, sis," Lila said, taking a step closer and handing her a simple pink shift-dress.

Lexi took it, but was still dizzy, her head fuzzy. She took a step back to stay upright. Threw her arms out for good measure. Almost dropped the garment.

Angus hovered, prepared to catch her if she fell.

"Move, you giant oaf," his wife said, but there was affection in her voice. "I'll help her get dressed. I can keep her on her feet."

Her brother capitulated, and Lila's warm hands were quick and efficient, like the physician she was.

"My turn," Angus said.

The soft pink fabric tickled the tops of Lexi's feet when her older brother took a step forward and cupped her face, making her meet his gaze again.

Angus whispered a spellword and her head cleared immediately, no longer hazy or chaotic.

It was like the clouds moving away to reveal the sun. She could concentrate. She could think again.

Her brother hadn't released her yet. He caressed her cheeks, and smiled softly. "I've missed ye, troublesome lassie."

Lexi blew out a breath, flashed a smile of thanks and threw her arms around her brother. "I missed ye, too, ye giant oaf," she whispered.

He smelled good, like sandalwood, horses and new

leather, the true scents of home.

Angus chuckled, and she felt in rumble from his chest against her torso, as well as heard it.

The urgent reason for her arrival back in 1694 bubbled to the surface.

"How long?" Lexi demanded.

Concern darted across her brother's handsome face, and he threw a look to his wife. "I dinnae know," Angus admitted.

"Alana sensed the Stones opening, and we came to get you. That was less than ten minutes ago, if it helps," Lila added.

"Lexi, what's wrong?" Her brother asked, frowning.

Lexi hiked her now-unfamiliar skirts and started up the ridge from the beach without answering. However, their footsteps on the rough ground behind her shouted they'd followed.

Her heart leapt when her eyes landed on her silver mare, Turadh, who waited next to her brother's mare, Magda. Only two horses, so Lila must've ridden with her husband.

Lexi rushed to her mare, who whinnied a welcome. "Ah, lassie, I've missed ye. I've no time ta appreciate ye." She hugged her horse for two heartbeats, then climbed astride her wide back.

"Lexi, wait!" Lila shouted as she and Angus crested the ridge.

"Lass—" Her brother waved a hand.

"I dinnae have time ta wait! I need Mother's help!" She urged Turadh around and put her knees to the horse's sides, bolting forward like a stormy gale.

chapter twenty-two

The race to Dunvegan Castle she'd always known was faster than she'd ever ridden in her life. She should apologize to Turadh for pushing the mare so hard.

They galloped through the open gates, ignoring the guards. More than one MacLeod man-at-arms shouted after her, but she didn't pause.

She slid off her horse and left her in the bailey, not waiting for her cousin, Cormac, to meet her. The head of the castle men-at-arms was headed her way, but she rushed into the castle instead of acknowledging him. She didn't wait for any of the stable lads to take her horse, either.

Most of her family already assembled in the great hall, no doubt waiting for her to return with Angus and Lila—neither of whom had made it back yet.

Her father swept her up into a hug she didn't have time for, although his large body was warm and secure. She'd always felt safe in his strong embrace. He smelled like leather and sage, bringing her back to her childhood for just a moment. The laird was dressed in a plaid and a saffron leine, and that was also pleasing and familiar.

Lexi's aunts, uncles and cousins hovered around them, and she immediately felt smothered again, like before she'd left. She wanted to shout for all of them to back away, to give her space to breathe, but she'd already hurt her mother, and they weren't doing anything wrong.

They just loved her.

The deafening chatter and countless questions they posed were too hard to process, let alone answer.

Lexi's purpose in coming home was too dire.

"Let her go, Alex."

Uncle Xander's deep voice was muffled, since her ear was against her father's wide, muscled chest, covered by a saffron leine, but she could've kissed him.

"Something's very wrong," the former Fae Warrior said.

Xander could read minds without concentrating or casting a spell, and this was one time Lexi thanked the stars for his ability to invade her thoughts.

Her uncle always shared how much he disliked his gift most of the time, referring to it as a curse often. She didn't blame him. Hearing everyone's thoughts all the time had to be taxing.

When her mother read thoughts, it was with a spell, not a natural gift like Xander's.

Her father set her away from him, but kept his hands on her shoulders and squeezed gently. "Lass?" His long dark hair curtained his handsome face, and his expression was worried, his brow drawn tight.

She met his blue eyes, which were so much like her brother's. "I need my mother."

"I'm right here." Alana's voice turned the family's heads collectively as she descended the stairs and crossed the great hall.

Lexi broke away from her father, met the woman who'd birthed her halfway, throwing her arms around her. "*Mamaidh. Mamaidh,* I'm so sorry fer what I said tha' day. I dinnae mean—"

Alana cupped her face and their eyes met. "You were right, *mo chridhe.* You are a grown woman, and I have treated you like a bairn. You are a bairn no longer, even if you will always be *my* bairn." Her mother's violet eyes were misty, her smile so soft.

Shock rolled over her, and Lexi froze to the spot like steel swords pinning her feet to the ground. Her mother's reaction stole all the words from her mouth.

"I just can't bear the thought of losing you." Alana's voice wobbled.

Lexi swallowed. Hard. "Ye..." She cleared her throat and tried again, a giant lump lodging the words like a vault. "Ye dinnae need worry. Ye dinnae lose me. E'er, *Mamaidh.* I love ye."

"I love you, too, *mo chridhe.*"

They sobbed against each other, and the years of miscommunication and misunderstanding seemed to melt away.

Her heart ached with love, relief and wonder, all at the same time.

How she'd hurt her relationship with her mother over the years wasn't lost on her, either. Lexi was far from perfect, and the fault and hard feelings did not completely rest at Alana's feet alone.

They were too much alike, as her father always declared.

She hadn't seen it, or been able to agree.

Until now.

Until Graeme and Gramps.

Lexi pushed away gently, wiping the tears from her eyes.

Her mother stared, maintaining her gaze. "What is it, my love?"

"I need ye, Mother. I need yer help."

"What can I do?"

"'Tis no' fer myself. I need ye ta save Graeme's grandfa."

"Nay." Her father cut his hand through the air to illustrate his absolute denial. "Yer all mad. My daughter has finally returned ta us. She will stay here. 'Tis the way 'twill be. She is back where she belongs, wit' her family."

Her mother started to speak, but her father glared.

"Alana, dinnae try me. No' this time."

"Da—"

"Nay, lad." Her father shut her brother down before Angus was able to get any other words out.

Her brother and Lila had made it back to the great hall when Lexi was in her mother's arms. She'd quickly explained what'd happened to James MacDonald, that his heart was failing and the doctor from the future said nothing was to be done.

After a few questions from her surgeon sister-by-marriage, the woman confirmed the modern ailment of the heart was impossible to fix. Nothing could be done.

Lexi's despair returned, threatening to swallow her whole.

"'Tis my decision. She stays," he reaffirmed. He was not Alex, her father, he was Alex the Laird MacLeod, and although her mostly even-tempered da rarely got this way, he was a stubborn MacLeod, and when he made a decision, it was hard to sway him.

Her mother spoke again, tapping into her own royal attitude, but Alex merely repeated his hard, "Nay."

Lexi watched them all argue, tears in her eyes, and her heart thundering in her ears.

She didn't have time for this.

She needed to get back to Graeme and Gramps.

No matter that her world had tipped on its end.

It really was surreal. Her mother on her side for once, her father unequivocally opposed.

"Alex!" Uncle Duncan's shout gathered the family's collective attention.

Aunt Claire stood with their three sons next to him, her hands on her little cousin Iain's shoulders.

Everyone quieted, but her father harrumphed and crossed his arms over his massive chest, his mouth a hard line.

Normally, if not her mother, only Uncle Duncan, her father's twin, could make her father see reason, but the laird currently seemed unmoved by his brother.

Lexi sucked in a huge breath and held it to gather her courage. She took a step closer. "I love him, Da." She'd wanted to shout it, but her statement fell from her mouth as a broken whisper.

"Lassie..." Her father's face softened, but his blue

eyes were still hard sapphires. More the laird that wouldn't abide being questioned, than understanding father.

She had to plow forward. "His grandfa...he's like mine own."

"She speaks the truth, my love," Alana reached for her, but addressed her husband.

Lexi wasn't upset her mother pulled that information from her mind. Maybe it had been from the day they'd argued, maybe it was from today.

It didn't matter. Alana was on her side, and the feeling was unexpectedly comforting.

Lexi slid her hand into her mother's, and they moved even closer to her father, together. "They took me in, withou' question, when I arrived in their time, Da. Been takin' care a'me the whole time. Graeme kep' me safe."

She wasn't ready to admit more—although if she told her father she was no longer innocent, it might move him to charge into Faery Stones sword drawn.

"Like ye love my mother, Da, I love Graeme MacDonald."

Alex crushed his eyes shut. He dropped his arms to his sides, but he closed the small distance remaining between them, cupping her face. "Och, my lassie. A man from the far future? 'Tis no' what I wanted fer ye."

Tears burned her eyes and so many things she wanted to say pushed against her lips, but Lexi couldn't tell her father Graeme had never told her he loved her. It wouldn't help sway him.

She wanted to declare that she wanted nothing

more than to stay by Graeme's side forever, but it wouldn't likely help, either.

Lexi cleared her throat to find her voice. "I know, Da." She shrugged, still in his gentle hold. "I dinnae mean fer it ta happen. But I love him. I love his grandfa, too. Please, Da. Please let Mother try ta save him. Graeme dinnae need lose his grandfa, like I lost mine."

It was a low blow, really, because her father didn't likely want or need a reminder of losing his father. He'd always been close to the retired Laird MacLeod, and the loss had hit him worse than the rest of the family, although he'd held it all inside, as MacLeod men were prone to do.

"I'll go," Uncle Xander said.

His wife, Aunt Janet, her father and Uncle Duncan's sister, grabbed his arm and whispered something. Their son, her cousin Liam, stood close to his mother.

The tall, former Fae Warrior nodded, kissed his wife's cheek, then proceeded to stare her father down.

Lexi wanted to hug him.

"I have healing magic and a sword. I'll protect them."

She wanted to assure her uncle there was no need for protection with a sword in the far future, but her father released her and stepped forward.

"Ah, there'll be no need for tha'."

Lexi's heart sank to her toes. He wasn't going to allow her mother to save Gramps. New tears burned her eyes.

Alex grabbed his wife's hand, then reached for her. She let her father take her hand, her pulse thundering in her ears.

He smiled and met her eyes, but there was no humor in it. "I'm goin', too. I've some words fer this Graeme MacDonald."

chapter twenty-three

Where the hell was Lexi? Did she really have some sort of magic cure?

It'd been too long.

He paced the hallway outside of his grandfather's bedroom of his small home in Armadale.

After James MacDonald had rested a bit, he'd demanded to be released from the clinic in Dunvegan. Since the doctor had said it was only a matter of time, he'd agreed to release him on the conditions his grandfather retired. No more working, only rest.

"Call if there are any changes," Doc Guinn had said, and given Graeme his personal cellphone number. He'd probably make a house call if they needed him. "Please think over what I said about hospice."

Dammit.

Only a few steps from his hospital bed had his grandfather entirely winded, making the older man begrudgingly agree, and Graeme, along with Bridget's help, had managed to get him home and in bed.

That'd been yesterday. Lexi had disappeared without a trace. He'd found the blue truck on the road to the beach, not far from where he'd found her two weeks ago.

The keys had been left in the ignition, as if she'd

intended him to find it and take it back, but she was nowhere. No note, not a word.

Just gone.

Where the hell was she?

He'd looked into those earnest, concerned violet eyes when she'd asked, "Do ye trust me?" and of course, he'd said, "Yes." It was the only answer he could've mustered then, and it was true.

He *did* trust her.

As the hours ticked by, trusting only became more of a struggle.

His grief and fear for Gramps warred with the tiny kernel of hope from Lexi's declaration she could save him. All he could do was wait. And pray.

How was she going to save him?

What was she *not* telling him?

She had amnesia, right?

Lexi had pretty much confirmed Graeme's worst— always ignored—fears that she had secrets, but he couldn't guess at them now.

He had Gramps to worry about.

Bridget had cooked a few meals and he was grateful, but he'd also been glad when the pretty redhead left for the night and kind of dreaded her promise to return in the morning.

"Graeme, lad, stop pacin'."

He should be a little relieved that the codger's order from his bed sounded a little stronger, but Graeme's worry only spiked when he met the elderly man's dark eyes.

"I thought you were sleeping," he chided as he

entered the small room and crossed over to the bed.

His grandfather cursed in Gaelic, but offered a small smile—of all things—when he looked up. "I'm done sleepin'."

"No, sir, you need to rest."

One of those white bushy eyebrows arched, but James didn't answer, as if he didn't have the energy.

That scared the shit out of Graeme.

If the man couldn't shout anymore, it really was as bad as he feared.

His heart slid down into his stomach.

He sat at the bedside and wanted to take his hand, but didn't. They'd been getting along—starting a real relationship—and his gut hurt at the thought that it was all he'd have left.

Memories, and more loss.

"Ye look so much like him," his grandfather whispered, his tone almost wistful.

Graeme shifted on the chair.

The man gestured to a picture on the small bedside table. His hand shook when he lifted the frame, bringing it in for a closer look.

Why had he never noticed the framed photo before now?

In the faded image, his father stood in front of the house they were in now, a grin on his handsome face. He leaned against the green truck; his arms crossed over his chest.

A lump dominated Graeme's throat he had to swallow.

It was the truck his grandfather drove so Graeme

could drive the later model, blue one. In the photo, it looked new, and his father's pride leapt up from the old print.

He wasn't aware the green truck had been his dad's. When he'd tried to take it the first day they'd headed to Dunvegan Castle, the old man had barked at him to take the newer vehicle.

Maybe Gramps was attached to the green truck because it had belonged to his son.

His eyes smarted and he swallowed again. His chest was tight with the urge to rub the spot.

Graeme studied his father's face. So young and carefree. He'd probably been about twenty in the shot. His hair was darker than Graeme's—his mother a natural blonde, and he'd received her genes, but Gramps wasn't wrong. He could see himself in the man's face. Then again, Craig MacDonald had looked like *his* father, too.

"So do you," he croaked, so he wouldn't cry like a pussy. He leaned forward to replace the picture.

"Aye?"

Graeme nodded. "Yeah, MacDonald acorns don't fall far from the tree."

Gramps leaned his head back into his carved headboard and offered another small smile. "Ye and yer American sayin's." Fatigue deepened the lines on his face.

He pulled the pillows up so his grandfather's head wouldn't be directly on the wood, but the old man tried to shove his hands away.

"Gramps, are you okay? Do you want the oxygen?"

Doc Guinn had sent home a tank in case Gramps' lungs started to struggle like his heart.

"Nay, lad."

Graeme gritted his teeth. Seeing the man like this was too damn hard. After the hip surgery he'd been grumpy, uncooperative and defiant, but at least he hadn't lost his energy.

He'd take anger over *this*, any day.

"Gramps—"

"She'll be back. Dinnae worry yer head." His grandfather closed his eyes, but his smile was soft and sure.

"What?"

"Yer lass, she'll be back. All will be well."

"You know she left to save you?" Graeme touched Gramps' arm.

The man opened his dark eyes and met his gaze. "Hopin', more than anathin'. Did she say she could?"

He didn't want to acknowledge what he was too scared to believe, but he nodded anyway.

Gramps seemed to relax again, his shoulders loosening and his body sinking into the bed. "Then the lass will do as promised, even if we dinnae understand how."

"What do you mean?"

"The lass is Fae, lad. Proof of the Faery Folk."

Graeme blinked. "What?"

Maybe his grandfather was losing his mind, along with his failing heart.

"She came here from 1694, she tol' me herself," Gramps said.

"I think you're really tired —"

"Dinnae tell me what I am feelin'."

This demand was much more like his grandfather, and would've been a relief if the old man wasn't spouting nonsense that made Graeme consider calling Dr. Guinn for the name of a local psychiatrist. Was there even one on the isle?

"Gramps —"

"Dinnae use that tone wit' me, Graeme MacDonald."

He startled on the edge of his chair again. The shout was also normal-Gramps-like, but the man kept speaking, not giving him a chance to respond.

"The lass has magic; her mother is Fae. I saw her myself in the gardens of the big house. So bonnie she dinnae seem human. She came ta get yer lass, but Lexi refused to leave *ye*, I suspect. I dinnae ken how, but they all time-traveled from 1694, yer lass tol' me. Faery Folk are real. Magic is real."

Graeme couldn't help but reject every word from his mouth. Scotland was famous for their sentiments toward the spirit world, their Faeries, and certainly not uncommon for those of his grandfather's generation. Graeme's logic and practical view of the world just wouldn't let him share those beliefs.

The coughing fit that followed killed any retort he might've put forward.

"Gramps, stop talking." He reached for the cup of water next to his father's picture. "Drink. I think we should do the oxygen a bit."

His grandfather shook his head, but accepted the

cup and took a few sips. Then he cleared his throat and met Graeme's gaze with an intensity he shouldn't have had the strength for. "Believe me or no', ye will see. When the lass returns."

chapter twenty-four

raeme checked on his grandfather countless times the next hour as he slept, making sure he continued breathing and hadn't slipped away. He just couldn't leave the bedroom, let alone the cottage to return home for a shower and a change of clothes.

Eventually, his growling stomach pulled him into the kitchen in search of food. He peered in the refrigerator. He rejected the offerings Bridget had prepared and made himself a ham sandwich.

He didn't want to eat, but his body could use an energy boost. He forced the bread, meat, mustard and cheese down, bemoaning the fact Gramps didn't have a coffee pot. Lack of caffeine wasn't enough to tempt him to leave his grandfather alone.

A clattering noise from outside the back of the small house made him sit upright.

No one knocked, but he made his way through the kitchen and out into the tiny mudroom. He flipped on the outside light and opened the back door.

A familiar petite figure stood in Gramps' backyard.

His heart leapt. "Lexi! Oh, thank God!" A breath of relief flew out, and he snatched the woman he loved to his chest, covering her mouth in a kiss.

She snaked her arms around his neck and squeezed

him almost too-tight, kissing him back like always, with fervency and passion that zinged to all the places on his body they didn't have time to attend to right now.

Someone—sounding male—cleared his throat.

Graeme broke the lip-lock, but didn't let Lexi leave his arms—until he saw three people behind her. "Lexi? Who…?" He looked them up and down; a woman with two huge men flanking her.

Lexi slipped from his grip, and moved back a step.

The woman was petite, no taller than Lexi, and so gorgeous it took his breath away—even more so than his love.

Her face was ageless, and she had the same violet eyes as Lexi, but her hair a pale blonde. Platinum, really, long and probably past her hips if it weren't styled half-up in some sort of knot on the top of her head. Her dark purple dress made her eyes stand out even more. The light over the door played off the shiny, iridescent threat embroidered on the bodice.

The garment was odd though. Like something from a renaissance festival. It looked as if she'd stepped out of one of the paintings in the great hall of Dunvegan Castle.

The man on her left was huge, at least six and a half feet tall, with the same color hair and eyes—wasn't that some shit?

Including Lexi, three people with purple eyes?

His hair was short, and an honest-to-God sword hung from his belt. His off-white shirt was old-school, too, and his pants were of brown leather. His boots went all the way up to his knees. The image was more of a pirate without the eye-patch or parrot.

The other guy was equally tall, and dark-haired like Lexi. He openly glared at Graeme.

What was that about?

Graeme had never seen the man before in his life.

This man's sword was even bigger than the blond guy's, and strapped to his back. A kilt was wrapped around his waist, a yellow puffy-sleeved shirt tucked into it, but one shoulder was covered with the same plaid of the kilt, also tucked into his thick belt. The ties on his shirt hung open at his neckline.

This *had* to be a historical reenactment, the battle of William Wallace or something.

These guys made Graeme's six-foot-three seem puny. Even though he'd been a linebacker in college with his wide frame, he had nothing on the wall of muscle behind Lexi.

What the hell was going on?

Lexi's face was red, as if she was embarrassed, but she looked at him with a plea in her gorgeous eyes. "Graeme..." His name came out as a cracked whisper. "They're here to help your grandfa."

He stepped closer, and she reached for his hand.

Graeme had a whole lotta *what-the-fuck* going on, but he didn't deny her.

Lexi entwined their fingers. Her hand was shaking.

She hadn't answered his question.

"What do you mean? Who are they?"

He cheeks grew even redder, and she looked away.

"Tell him, love," the woman whispered. Her accent was Scottish, but it wasn't like Lexi's brogue. It was refined...formal. Like she was well-educated or rich.

Lexi's chest heaved with a huge breath, fortifying.

Graeme couldn't look away when she finally met his eyes. He was compelled to maintain eye contact, and he wanted to know what the hell was going on.

Now.

"This is my mother, an' my Uncle Xander." She gestured to the two fair-haired people. "They're…healers. The last…'tis my father."

Shock rolled over him, and he reared back. "What?"

"I…"

"Lexi, you remember them? When did your memories come back? How? What happened?" He looked from the three strangers and back to the only woman he'd ever loved. "Or…is this something else?" He swallowed. "Why…why are they dressed like they just stepped out of a painting?"

"Lad—" the blond man started.

Graeme dropped Lexi's hand and slashed through the air with his. "No, not you." He pointed at the man, rude or not. "I'm asking *her*." Anger spiked up from his gut, and his face heated. He didn't spare the man another glance, and when his love's eyes welled with tears and spilled over, it took all he was made of not to snatch her to his chest again to comfort her.

His grandfather's crazy story about Lexi being a faery, or a time-traveler popped into his brain, as if it was holding a sign in front of his eyes, but he shut it down fast.

It's not possible.

The old man had to have been suffering from oxygen deprivation or something.

Lexi stood close enough to touch, but he just couldn't.

She was fully sobbing, and it was killing him.

Her *father* stepped toward him, his glare even more menacing than before, and he raised a thickly muscled arm, as if he was going to pull that giant sword from the leather encasing it.

"Alex," the blond man said, and grabbed the man's arm.

The ethereally beautiful woman also shot a glare at who Graeme assumed was her husband, then turned to Lexi, and closed the distance to her. She whispered something to her daughter, who nodded and went to her father.

The big man tugged her to him, and Lexi sobbed into his massive chest. He rubbed her back, like Graeme had done so many times he'd lost count, but his narrowed eyes never left Graeme.

She sure as hell didn't look as if she didn't know who these people were, or like she'd *just* remembered them.

Why was *she* crying?

He felt like an ass, but it wasn't like it was his fault.

Although, he suspected his reaction to this shit show was the reason for her tears, but what the hell else was he supposed to say?

No one would tell him what was going on.

Lexi's mother touched his wrist, and he jumped. "Let us have this discussion later. Alexandria fears your grandfather's illness is grave. Can you show us to him?"

Graeme didn't look away from the eyes so like

Lexi's.

The woman's words were soft, urgent, as if she really did give a shit about a man she didn't know. Her refined accent made him think of royalty for some reason.

His vision blurred and he called himself every name in the book.

He was crying? Like a pussy?

Over Lexi or Gramps?

The woman squeezed his arm, and he jolted back into his skin.

"N-n-no. Someone needs to tell me what the hell is going on!" Graeme tried to demand, but it came out a stuttered whisper.

The blond man stepped closer. "Lad, I know none of this makes sense right now. Let us help, if we can, then we will explain." His accent was like the woman's, Scottish, but not a Highland brogue.

He shook his head, but they'd been right about one thing; Gramps' condition was serious. "What can you do?" he whispered.

Lexi's mother's expression was so soft, so loving, he almost lost it again. "We dinnae know until we see him."

Graeme blinked at the familiar Scottish pronunciation, and had to stave off tears. He wanted to shut it all down. Deny every impossible word Gramps had said about Lexi and Fae Folk.

Then there was the time travel part.

He didn't want to face it, because all this meant something he'd denied every time it had entered his head.

Lexi *had* lied to him.

Nothing made sense, but what did he have to lose?

Could these people save his grandfather's life?

Graeme could let them try.

He sucked in a breath and met the woman's eyes again. She was really too gorgeous to be human, as Gramps had claimed, but faeries weren't real.

They couldn't be real.

However, he could also see Lexi in her features, and somehow that made his heart hurt.

Graeme led the two strangers to his grandfather's small bedroom.

Gramps looked small and sick in the bed, and it was only a twin-sized. He was tall, with wide shoulders like Graeme, but right then he looked tiny and old.

He tried not to gulp as they went inside and he hovered in the doorway.

James MacDonald wasn't asleep anymore. How could he with all the racket outside? When he saw the two fair-haired people, his expression lit up with a smile that took years off his weathered face, like he'd never seen him smile before.

Shock rolled over Graeme when Gramps reached for Lexi's mother, and she immediately gave him her hand.

The room was tiny, and Lexi's uncle made it seem even smaller as he hovered by the bed.

Lexi's mother started speaking in Gaelic, and his grandfather was on it, answering her every query in the same language, which only added to Graeme's sense of not knowing what the hell was going on.

She put her hands on his chest and closed her eyes. Said something aloud he didn't understand.

He wanted to demand a full explanation again — in English — but then Lexi's mother's hands started to glow. Like really freaking glow, the light emanating from her skin from the inside out.

Was this all a trick?

A ploy to make people think it was a miracle?

Graeme stepped into the room because his eyes had to be playing tricks on him.

The blond man lifted his head, but didn't turn toward him.

Lexi's mother's expression held the extreme concentration he'd seen on her daughter's face many times, when she'd been trying to accomplish something.

The recognition smarted.

After a few more tense moments, the glow died, and Lexi's mother met his gaze. "I believe we can help." She smiled, and he didn't miss the sweat dotting her forehead. "But I will require Alexandria."

Graeme blinked as more *what-the-fuck* danced around his head again.

She hadn't asked, but he'd heard the demand in her voice.

Go get Lexi.

The blond man nodded, as if he'd read his mind.

Graeme swallowed.

He didn't want to look at her, let alone speak to her or ask anything of her, but this was for Gramps. He might not understand what the hell was going on, but this was for his grandfather's life.

He did understand *that*.

Graeme retreated from the room and whirled, practically smacking into Lexi's father.

She stood next to the huge man, holding onto his arm, and they had obviously followed him into the house. Her pretty face was tear-streaked, her violet eyes red and swollen.

He told himself he didn't give a shit, and cleared his throat. "Uh, your mom said she needs you."

Lexi nodded, but her eyes bored into his. "Graeme—"

"If you can help my grandfather, please do," he snapped.

The huge man growled, a sound that made him want to retreat, but Graeme refused. Instead, he chose not to look directly at him, and to keep his focus only on Lexi.

Her splotchy skin from the tears he'd caused ripped at his insides, but he was too angry to reach for her, console her, touch her in some way. He was too hurt, his heart *and* his pride.

She'd made him feel like a fool.

"Lexi, you lied to me. For two weeks."

She sniffled, but nodded.

At least she wasn't trying to deny it.

"Alexandria, please come," her mother called from Gramps' room.

Her throat worked as she swallowed. That beautiful spot was so soft when he'd kissed her there, and the memory of her skin tasting like summer berries invaded his anger. Graeme cursed himself again.

She darted around him and her father, disappearing into the small room.

Graeme inadvertently met the man's eyes.

They were blue, not violet, and still promised violence.

Lexi's father didn't speak, but he did make another grunting-growl noise. He crossed huge muscular arms over an equally giant muscled chest.

Good sense whispered in the back of Graeme's mind that he should flee. However, he was not a small man, either, and this was his grandfather's home. *They* were the visitors. He stared Lexi's father down. After all, if the big guy wanted to kill him with that claymore, he'd have to move his arms, first.

"She dinnae wish me ta harm ye," the man gritted out, as if he'd read his mind. Lexi's dad's brogue rolled over him that sounded just like hers.

Graeme wanted to bark a sarcastic, *thanks?* but he didn't. Perhaps out of his sense of self preservation. The man did have a weapon, and he was the size of a small house.

He couldn't look at her father's glare anymore so he went back to the doorway, and put his hand on the frame.

If the three people who were supposedly *not* human had noticed his presence, there was no reaction.

All he could see of Gramps was his feet, because Lexi, her mother, and her uncle lined the side of the bed.

Lexi was between the two fair-haired people, and the three of them had linked hands. Her mother's free one was on his grandfather somewhere. The man, too, had one hand on Gramps at his ankle. He was bent forward slightly, because he was so tall.

The same unnatural glow from before turned even brighter now, as if his grandfather's body was made of light. The room also radiate warmth, coming toward him in gentle waves.

Gramps cried out with a strained voice.

Graeme surged forward to step them from hurting him.

A massive hand landed on his shoulder, immobilizing him with its size and power. "Let them work, lad. If my Alana said she can help yer grandfa, she can help him."

Graeme wanted to protest, yank away, storm the room, but something about the calmness in the man's voice penetrated his senses.

"Disturbin' 'em dinnae help matters," Lexi's dad added, his voice even lower. The man's eyes were so blue, like glinting sapphires, and finally void of the violence. This was the first time he wasn't looking at him with aggression and threats.

Even so, Graeme couldn't find the words to thank him, but the man gave a small nod, as if he understood, and he turned his attention back to the group.

He couldn't believe his own eyes. All of this...combined with what Gramps claimed about faeries and magic... No, this couldn't be real.

The glow brightened more, to a brilliant, blinding sun lighting up the entire room. Graeme had to shield his eyes as the light encased the figures, swallowing their shadows.

chapter twenty-five

▶▶ "It's all true, isn't it?" Graeme wobbled on his feet and the hallway started spinning. For some reason, his eyes smarted with tears again.

A huge hand again landed at the center of his back, but it was the only thing that kept him from landing on his ass on the hardwood floor.

"Aye, 'tis."

He was surprised the man cared enough to keep him on his feet. Graeme didn't know whether to laugh or cry. "How?"

"Magic," he said simply, as if that answered everything; explained everything.

He hated that all the math was adding up in his head about Lexi. When she'd seemed like she'd never seen a truck before on the beach two weeks ago, it was because she really *hadn't*.

She'd been so fascinated with cellphones, light switches, running water, microwaves, coffee, because she hadn't ever seen them before. When her mouth had hung open on the ferry, when she'd looked as if she'd never tasted ice cream, she really hadn't.

The day he'd found her, when she'd been so scared...now it all made sense.

He'd made her feel better.

He'd fallen in love with her, too.

That didn't matter.

"She lied to me," he spat, his earlier anger back and alive, shooting up from his gut.

Her father sighed, which was about the last thing he'd expected the man to do. "My lassie dinnae have a choice, lad."

"She did. There's *always* a choice." Graeme hated that the huge man looked at him with sympathy, compassion even. He almost would've preferred him to return to the vengeful, slaughtering expression.

He hated pity.

"Ye would ne'er have believed her, lad." His deep voice was even and reasonable, and Graeme didn't want to hear it.

"She *lied* to me," he repeated.

"Graeme MacDonald," the man retorted, but his last name came out as if Lexi's father was cursing instead of stating his surname.

"How is it you know *my* name, and I don't have a fucking clue about *yours*."

The man arched a dark eyebrow and his mouth rippled, as if he was amused?

Graeme had just cursed at him.

How was that funny?

"Alex MacLeod." Lexi's father thrust his hand out for a shake.

He stared at the big paw before he grabbed it, but he finally capitulated, and the man gave him a firm, but not crushing, shake.

Alex's hand was calloused and strong, suggesting

the claymore wasn't just for show.

Graeme looked him up and down, and tried to be subtle about it. The guy had to be north of fifty, but he looked younger, not to mention his muscles were like some meathead who lived in the gym.

"My lass tol' me ye been takin' care a' her, and I'm grateful. Thank ye for seein' ta her safety."

"It wasn't a chore." Truth tumbled out. Regret at his choice of words hit him with one look at the man's expression.

His demise was back in the blue depths.

He might as well have said, *"Well she's gorgeous when she's naked."*

"I believe ye, especially wit' what I was the unfortunate witness ta upon our arrival." The man's tone was dry.

Yeah, he'd kissed the crap out of her in front of her parents, hadn't he?

Graeme smirked, but then the hurt at her deception reignited his anger, and he glared at her father. "It doesn't change anything. She *lied* to me. We were together every day for two weeks. There were countless moments to tell the truth."

"Had my lass tol' ye from *when* she hailed, would ye have believed her?" There was a dare in those sapphire eyes.

Graeme shook his head. "It doesn't matter."

"Nothin' matters more," Alex said quickly.

There was no way he was actually standing here, reasoning with a man who was really from the seventeenth century.

He had to be dreaming, or have lost his mind.

People's hands and bodies didn't really glow.

People certainly didn't travel through time.

There was no such thing as a faery.

For about the hundredth time of the day, his eyes smarted with tears he definitely wouldn't shed in front of this man.

When Graeme looked back into Alex's face, not only did he see Lexi there, he read compassion again, and he couldn't deal with it.

He whirled away from the man and glanced back into his grandfather's bedroom. The glow was dimming, and he wanted to ask what it meant, but didn't get the chance.

Lexi's mother wobbled, and went down. Her body crumpled by the side of the bed.

"Alana!" Alex shoved Graeme from the doorway to get into the room, immediately dropping to the floor to cradle his wife.

"*Mamaidh!*" Lexi shouted, hovering over her parents.

Graeme couldn't take it anymore. He rushed into the room.

"I'm fine, loves," her mother said, but her voice was weak, exhausted. "Magic is so contrary in this time; it took a great deal from me."

"Gramps?" Graeme breathed.

"He is well. Sleeping," Lexi's uncle answered. Sweat dotted the man's face and he pulled a handkerchief from a pouch on his belt and blotted his forehead. The lines on his pale skin said he was tired, too, but he didn't look as fatigued as Lexi's mom.

Graeme swallowed against the huge lump suddenly dominating his throat. He didn't know what do to first. He scanned his grandfather's form in the bed.

The color had returned to the older man's cheeks, and for the first time in weeks, he did look peaceful. His forehead felt cool to the touch, not feverish or clammy. His chest rose and fell at regular intervals.

He really was just sleeping.

The stupid tears spilled over, and Graeme didn't care. He looked at the tall man, then Lexi's parents. "Thank you so much. I...I can't repay you. I wouldn't know how." He didn't understand how they'd done it, but Gramps *was* healed.

Graeme didn't want to look at Lexi.

Somehow, he couldn't.

Her mother smiled. She seemed to rest comfortably in Alex's arms, against that massive chest, and pink had returned to her cheeks, although her skin was the same alabaster as her daughter's. "Your care for my daughter is repayment enough, Graeme MacDonald." Her voice was stronger, too.

"Can I get you guys something? Water? Food?"

Lexi's mother smiled again. It was warm and loving, and it made his stomach jump. "Xander and I would be grateful for some water, aye. Thank you."

When Graeme returned to the room with two glasses of water, one glance at Gramps told him the older man was still out, and all members of Lexi's party were on their feet.

He still didn't want to look at her, because every

word her father had said in the hallway made way too much sense he didn't want to face.

Had the gorgeous naked woman on the beach said, *"Hi, I'm from 1694,"* Graeme might still have taken her to the clinic, but asked for the nearest psych ward.

He wouldn't have believed she'd time-traveled, and that wasn't taking to consideration the Fae of it all.

Her mother thanked him for the water, something the tall blond guy echoed.

Graeme made his way to his grandfather's bedside, and brought over the same chair he'd occupied before Lexi and her family had arrived. He studied the man's face. Somehow, Gramps looked younger, and the creases in his forehead that seemed permanent were now considerably lessened. Like he wasn't in pain anymore.

How long would he sleep?

"He'll wake naturally. He is not under a sleep spell." Again, Lexi's uncle was the one to speak.

Sleep spell?

What the hell was that?

Wait, he hadn't asked that question *aloud*, had he?

"Xander can read minds," Lexi said quietly.

The *what-the-hell* expression must've risen on his face again.

He could feel her gaze on him.

Graeme finally looked at her, and immediately wished he hadn't.

Her eyes were swollen and red from crying, and she looked tired — well, haggard, really. She had a pallor he didn't like, and her shoulders were slumped.

The tears were because of him.

Guilt leapt up from his gut and warred with his waning anger, but also threw in a new side of confusion.

"Wait. What? He can read minds?"

The man nodded when Graeme met the purple gaze so much like his lover's.

Damn, he shouldn't have thought that last word. Not to mention any of the other lovely crap that had darted through his brain since he'd come into this room.

Like how much she'd enraptured him the last two weeks. Along with everything else she'd done. *They'd* done together.

"Uh, lad…" the uncle started. "I can read yours right now."

Graeme froze.

Of all the things that had gone through his mind since they'd come into this room…

All of it had been overheard?

Fabulous.

The smirk the guy wore pretty much shouted he'd heard all *that,* too.

He was also too good-looking to be human. It hadn't occurred to Graeme until right then, but it wasn't like he was in the business of checking out dudes.

"Your grandfa should be well now. He should rest for several days, but his heart is no longer damaged," Lexi's mother said.

Alex had one arm around her shoulders, and she was tucked into his side, something Graeme had often done with Lexi.

He…hurt…when he looked at *her.*

He loved her.

It wasn't like a switch he could turn off, no matter if the woman he'd fallen for had lied to him. Even if it was a huge lie.

Alex's words teased his mind again.

Her father was right.

He wouldn't have believed her.

At. All.

Lexi had done what she'd needed to navigate a time so different than her own. When he thought about it like that, Graeme was actually in awe of her.

She should've been constantly freaked the hell out and screamed about, well—everything. The truck, electricity, running water, the stove. Especially the ferry.

Instead, she'd adapted. She even cooked. More than his own in-the-microwave cooking skills. She'd learned to drive, too.

She's stronger than I ever could be.

Lexi had been clever to cover her lack of knowledge with amnesia, but then again, that'd been *Graeme's* assumption, hadn't it? She'd just gone with it, and who could blame her?

Not to mention, she'd found a way to save his grandfather's life when modern medicine said it wasn't possible.

"Lexi," Graeme whispered. He stood from the chair, and a shudder shot down his spine. He rammed his hand through his hair.

Her eyes were glued to his face, and the hope he read in her expression made his heart slide down to his toes.

"You saved him. He's alive because of you... of your

family. Lexi—" His eyes burned, and a new tear spilled over, but Graeme didn't care to hold it back anymore.

Lexi had tears on her cheeks again, too. She shrugged. "I love him." Then she shoved her hands into the pockets of her jeans, and it was so normal, so modern, he smirked.

"I love you," he blurted.

She gasped. A moment later, more tears ran down her cheeks.

Her mother whispered something to her father and uncle.

Alex grunted, but allowed his wife to lead him down the hallway, Xander on their heels.

Graeme was half-surprised the big man had agreed to leave, especially after his declaration regarding the man's daughter.

He didn't really need the privacy. He didn't care if the whole world knew how he felt about Alexandria MacLeod, even if she was over three hundred years old.

They weren't really alone anyway, with Gramps in the room, but his grandfather hadn't stirred.

"Say that again." Lexi's voice was low, yet commanding.

She was her father's daughter.

He chuckled and shook his head. "C'mere, darlin'." He opened his arms and pulled her to him.

Lexi didn't fight him, but she wouldn't let him tuck her all the way into his chest. "Graeme." His name was a demand.

He caressed her cheek, and looked into her gorgeous violet eyes. "I love you, Alexandria MacLeod."

More tears spilled, and he thumbed them away before they could crest her cheekbones.

"It must be bad news." He whispered the tease.

"Nay." She shook her head. "Nay. Ne'er that. I love ye, too, Graeme MacDonald."

He dipped down and took her mouth.

Like always, Lexi didn't disappoint, slipping her arms around his neck.

Graeme urged her flush against him, as close as he could get her, and he kissed her until his head spun, until he couldn't breathe and his cock was hard and aching.

Sense finally dawned on him that his grandfather was only a few feet away. Not to mention Lexi's father was down the hall, still in possession of that huge sword.

He broke away from her tempting mouth, resting his forehead against hers.

Her warm, ragged breaths caressed his cheeks and Graeme wanted to kiss her again. That was only made worse when he took in her crimson flush, and heavy-lidded eyes.

Lexi was as lost in him as he was in her, and he couldn't get enough of it.

That certainly hadn't changed.

"I love you," he whispered again, as if now that he'd said it once, he couldn't keep it in if he tried.

Her grin was brilliant and had his heart at a canter all over again.

"An' I love ye. So damn much."

Graeme chuckled. "Don't cuss, or your dad will kill me for being a bad influence."

"He'd likely lop off yer bollocks fer touchin' me

a'fore he did fer somethin' ye said."

He blinked.

She wasn't kidding.

"Actually, I need to thank him."

"Aye?" She arched an elegant ebony eyebrow.

"Yeah. Your dad explained everything. In a way I understand better, I think."

"*My* da?" Her voice cracked.

Graeme nodded. "He was right, darlin'. If you'd told the truth from the start, I wouldn't have believed you."

Mixed emotions darted across her gorgeous face. "I'm sorry I lied ta ye. I dinnae want ta, but—"

"I know, Lexi. You did what you had to. I understand, I really do."

"I dinnae lie ta hurt ye."

He nodded and reached for her again, because where she was concerned, he couldn't keep his hands to himself. It'd been that way from the start.

"I dinnae make a practice a' lyin'."

Graeme kissed her nose, and smiled. "I know. I believe that. Besides, your lie is nothing compared to what you've done for me and Gramps. I'll never be able to make it up to you—and your family—for saving him."

"Ye can."

"I can?"

"Aye, by lovin' me."

He grinned. "Done."

Lexi flashed another bright smile and his whole body zinged, as if she'd touched him again.

"Can I ask you something?"

She cocked her head to one side. "Anathin'."

"You're a faery? Like a real one?"

Lexi's mouth rippled with amusement and again, Graeme barely resisted kissing her. Maybe she'd cast a spell on him.

"My mother is — was — a Fae princess. My father is human."

"A princess?"

"Aye. 'Tis a long story."

"Tell me some time?"

She smiled and nodded.

Graeme cupped her cheeks again, caressing her alabaster skin with his thumbs. "1694, huh?"

She nodded, but didn't dislodge his gentle hold. Lexi turned her face and kissed his palm.

"How did I let you get away with it for two whole weeks?" he whispered.

Another smiled played at her delectable mouth. "Magic?"

Graeme picked her up and swung her around. "Well, Alexandria MacLeod, you certainly did put me under some kind of spell, that's for sure." He set her down, pressed a kiss to her forehead, and whirled away, striding from his grandfather's room.

"Where're ye goin'?" Lexi asked.

"To ask your dad if I can marry you. That's how things are done, aren't they?"

chapter twenty-six

arry me?

Lexi gasped.

Her American from the future wanted to marry her.

The giddiness was almost too overwhelming, and she could barely breathe from the elation bubbling up her throat.

"Graeme, wait!" She hurried to match his much longer stride.

Just as he reached the sitting room, she grabbed the back of his shirt and pulled hard.

Her beautiful MacDonald turned his pretty midnight eyes on her.

Lexi sucked in a breath, and her tummy jumped.

He *loved* her.

He'd told her so.

Three times.

"What is it, darlin'?" His brow was low and tight.

"Yer assumin' I'd wed ye, an' ye neglected ta ask *me*." She thumbed her chest.

That stopped him in his tracks. His eyes went wide. His mouth opened to speak but no sound came out.

Then he flashed a smile that made her insides flutter.

"I want you to have my babies. I figured your father would prefer we be married first. Especially since you said he'd to lop off my bollocks."

Lexi's heart stuttered, skipped a beat and stumbled back to a normal rhythm. She bit her lip to keep from laughing. "Graeme." She tried to say his name like a warning, but some of her joy had bubbled up, turning her voice breathier than she liked when she was trying to make a point. She perched her hands on her hips instead.

The grin he flashed told her the man she loved saw right through her.

He put his hands through her bent arms, grabbed her waist, and tugged her to him. Graeme was still grinning. "You have to marry me. I love you. That's really all there is to it."

"I still dinnae hear a question." She tried to sound stern.

His chuckle was endearing.

This man knew how to light her up inside.

"You're it for me, Lexi. No matter what year you come from, you're here with me now, and I want it to stay that way." He took a breath, and his expression was so loving, so sincere. "Alexandria MacLeod, will you marry me?"

Her breath caught, even though she'd expected the question. She just hadn't anticipated how those words would make her feel. Lexi quivered from the inside out. She bit her lip to stave off the wave of emotions.

She'd lied to him for two weeks, but he'd not only forgiven her, he told her he loved her. Repeatedly. Now, he was asking her to wed him?

Stay with him in the future?

It was all she'd ever wanted.

That, and the bairns he'd mentioned.

Lexi threw herself into Graeme's arms.

He caught her up, like he always had, like he always would.

Graeme kissed her, their tongues dancing and dueling until her body was on fire for him.

"Is that a yes?" He breathed against her lips.

"Aye," she panted, grabbing his shirt with both hands so she could stay on her feet. Her belly was hot, and her legs were mush.

She forced a deep breath, and to calm her excitement. She still had to tell her parents what she wanted.

Pray they accepted it.

Accepted Graeme.

Their gazes brushed and locked. "I know it's a lot to ask. It's really not fair, considering your whole family lives in the seventeenth century." Graeme's expression was sad and serious. "Your family loves you, Lexi, so—"

"Ye an' Gramps are my family, too."

He blew out a breath and kissed her knuckles, but he still radiated a touch of sadness.

"I've magic. We can go home any time."

"We?"

She nodded. "Aye, I'd love fer ye ta meet my whole family."

"If all the guys in your family are as big as your dad

and uncle—I dinnae know if I'd survive."

Lexi burst out laughing at his attempt at her Scottish brogue. "Weeel, my brother an' my Uncle Duncan are. My cousins are braw, aye, but still growin'."

"You have another uncle?"

"Aye, my da's twin."

"Do they look very much alike?"

"Oh, aye, verra much."

Graeme gave an overdramatic sigh, but offered her his arm and flashed a smile. "C'mon, darlin' I still have to ask your dad that question."

Lexi's da stared Graeme down stoically.

Which was better than she'd assumed he'd take the news—brandishing his claymore.

A long, hard moment later, Alex looked away from her newly betrothed, and commanded all her attention.

"'Tis truly what ye desire, my lassie?" Her father asked gently, cupping her cheeks. His blue eyes, so full of love and worry, raked her face.

"Aye, Da. I love him. He loves me. I want nothin' more than ta wed him an' stay here."

Her mother stood very close, tears in her eyes, but Lexi felt in her heart—maybe in her soul—that Alana would respect her wishes this time.

"I do, sir. Love her, I mean. Very much," Graeme added, but Alex didn't acknowledge him.

"Ye'll be leavin' all ye've ever known, *mo chridhe*."

"Da, I've already learned so much since I've been

here," Lexi whispered. She wanted both her parents to know she would be okay in the far future, because of Graeme.

Her mother wrested her gently from her father's grip, and enfolded her into a hug.

Graeme MacDonald is your fate, my love. Instead of speaking aloud, her mother put the words in her head, as if she couldn't bear to speak them.

Lexi smiled and burrowed into her mother's hold.

"You're my bonnie braw, lass, and you always have been, my love. I now know you'll be fine, and you belong in this time," her mother whispered.

"I love ye, *Mamaidh*," she breathed on a sob.

Her father wrapped his arms around them both, and Lexi let her parents hold her, like she hadn't since she was a wee thing.

She inhaled deeply, memorizing their scents.

Uncle Xander looked on, his expression stoic, as was not uncommon for him, but his eyes held emotions she wanted to look away from.

I'll miss ye, too.

He smiled gently, letting her know he'd heard her thought.

This wasn't a sad thing.

It wasn't a forever.

She would see her family again.

He is a good man. Like her mother had done, Xander's voice was in her head, not in her ears.

I think so, too.

"*Mamaidh*, Da, I'll see ye again," Lexi said. "'Tis no such thing as goodbye with magic."

Her mother smiled. Her violet eyes still shone with tears, but she didn't look so sad.

Lexi kissed her cheek and slipped into her uncle's waiting arms.

Xander lifted her from the ground and hugged her tight. "Be well, lass." He kissed her forehead. "Mayhap with you here, my lad will cause less trouble."

She flashed an unrepentant grin. Over the years, she and Liam had gotten into more mischief than all three of her Uncle Duncan and Aunt Claire's sons—which was saying something, because the middle child, Rory, was made of trouble.

Her uncle tweaked her nose. "That's nothing to be proud of, lassie."

Lexi smiled again, but didn't retort.

Her father stalked to her beloved. "It matters no' tha' centuries separate us. If ye hurt her, I will kill ye. I've magic on my side." Alex threw his finger in Graeme's face, as if thrusting a sword.

"Da!" She dashed to him, tugged on his arm, but her father was made of iron.

"Had ta be said."

Instead of running away, Graeme looked Alex square in the eyes and gave a curt nod. "Fair enough." He thrust his hand out for a shake.

Her uncle chuckled and shook his head.

Her father arched an eyebrow, then a slow smile etched across his face. He clasped his arm, instead of shaking his hand, a greater show of respect, acceptance and affection.

Tears sprang to her eyes again.

"We shall go," her mother said softly, but she seemed at peace, her beautiful face placid.

"Will ye accompany us ta the Faery Stones?" her father asked, looking at Lexi, then to Graeme.

"I think I've had enough magic for one day," he replied, shaking his head. "Go, if you need to say goodbye there. I'll wait for you here," he whispered in her ear and kissed her cheek.

Her mother hugged him.

Graeme looked a little surprised, but held the former princess close.

"Dinnae let her order you around, Graeme MacDonald. My daughter can be more than a handful," her mother murmured.

Her betrothed grinned.

Lexi wanted to stick her tongue out, like she would've when she was wee. However, she'd won major ground today and picking her battles seemed more important.

"I've one condition," her father announced.

"Da—" she complained, but he plowed on, as if she hadn't started to speak.

"Ye, Graeme MacDonald, will bring my daughter home ta wed her. I dinnae intend ta miss my only lass' weddin'."

"Yes, sir. I wouldn't have it any other way."

Lexi gasped.

"Truly? You're willin' to travel through time ta marry me?" She threw her arms around Graeme.

He caught her up.

Always.

"I'll marry you through every single year that passes from 1694 to here if I have to."

Lexi let her love pull her even closer and take her mouth.

"Let us away, I dinnae desire ta witness the like of *this* again." Her father groused, scowling.

epilogue

A few months later…

Ounvegan Castle, version 1694, circled above Graeme's head as he marveled at the great hall. Something he never could've imagined he'd actually see in person, in real life. He was as amazed by it, as Lexi had been by the modern-day version. The rustic beauty in every single corner was missing in the twenty-first century, and he loved it instantly. He didn't know where to look first.

Several huge candle-lit chandeliers hung from the ceiling and gave off a nice ambient glow, while also offering enough light in the huge space. The tables faced the other direction from what he'd known, and they were rough-hewn dark wood instead of refined furniture; it reminded him of the Harry Potter movies. The charming glow of a large room that felt more intimate and cozier than one expected. Plenty of chairs and long benches provided enough space to feed a small army.

His master restoration specialist of a grandfather inspected everything as close as he could get, putting his face right up to each feature of the castle, including stairwells and walls. The man looked like a kid who'd just woken up in Santa's workshop, with his every wish at his fingertips.

Graeme felt like he'd stepped onto the set of some historical movie, like Braveheart, or something. Had to restrain himself from looking for cameras and boom microphones.

He and Gramps looked like characters starring in that movie, too, dressed in clothing from Lexi's time. Her father and brother had met them with period-appropriate clothing at the cave where a bunch of crystals had transported them back in time.

Even if they'd managed to bring clothing to 1694 — which they couldn't, they both had landed naked — their jeans and T-shirts wouldn't have matched with the time period. Not only that, apparently it wasn't common knowledge that several members of Clan MacLeod were Fae. It was widely suspected, but something the family didn't want confirmed. It was too dangerous for them all.

Time travel was certainly…something.

Alana had made it so they didn't have to experience the normal disorientation after crossing centuries by using her magic. They hadn't been tossed to the beach, like Lexi had when she'd come forward the first time, but it was some kind of spell Graeme didn't understand.

The Faery Stones were a wonder he could never describe, so it was a good thing he wasn't allowed.

His grandfather seemed to take it much more in stride than Graeme ever expected. Like going back in time at a whim was a normal thing, like visiting a theme park or going on vacation.

Hell, maybe it would become a normal thing for

them now.

The kilt they gave Graeme—or a plaid, as Lexi's family called it—been an adventure to don. After a full year living in Scotland, no one had ever told him for a man to wear it properly, he had to lay down on the floor and roll into it like a burrito. At least the old school version.

Gramps opted for what Alex had called trews, which were just pants a tad too tight for Graeme's liking. The older man wore an olive-colored puffy-sleeved shirt called a leine, that hung down over the kilt's waist, not tucked in like in modern times.

The one Graeme wore was off-white, borrowed from Lexi's brother, Angus. The guy was a few inches taller than him, like the laird and his brother, but it worked.

Angus had helped Graeme get dressed in the historical clothing and prepared him for the time-period wedding. The nice conversation he shared with his soon-to-be brother-in-law, and his wife, Lila, gave him hope that all of this would actually work.

The whole family was amazing. What astonished him even more was Lexi's sister-in-law, Lila, as well as her Aunt Claire, were from the twenty-first century, both from Texas.

If that didn't blow his mind enough, like him, they were from the Dallas area. For a further mind-twister, they'd arrived in the seventeenth century about twenty years apart, but had been born within a few years of each other in the twenty-first. Lila only had a few years on Graeme, but Claire was almost fifty.

"Don't try to process it," Lexi's aunt said. She patted his arm and smiled softly. "'Twill just make your brain hurt."

"You're right." He smiled and took a breath. "So, Lexi told me your sister's here, too? That she married the, uh…the MacDonald laird?"

"Yup, they should be here soon. Do me a favor, don't mention that Armadale in your time is in ruins, okay? Duncan has a tendency ta gloat that Dunvegan is still around, an' as much as I love the man, he can be an ass." She gestured to where her husband and Alex stood, chatting with Gramps at the hearth.

It was not doubled, like the one they'd finished their work on, about a week after his grandfather had recovered. It was still wide and deep, and currently sported a friendly fire.

Lexi had been right. Her dad and his twin, Duncan, were identical, and he couldn't have told them apart if someone had paid him. He was completely clean-shaven, while Alex wore a trimmed beard, but it was the only distinguishing feature. Although, the laird had been cleanshaven the night they'd met, so maybe facial hair wasn't a regular thing for either of them.

Dr. Guinn considered James MacDonald's full recovery nothing less than miraculous. Gramps had refused to be examined for a few weeks, but then the doctor showed up on his doorstep for a house call.

They — of course — couldn't admit that it actually *had* been a bit of a miracle. Or a magi-cal.

Graeme chuckled and winked at his soon-to-be-wife's aunt. "Okay, no worries." He cocked his head to one side. "Your sister has a daughter, right?"

"Aye," she said. Her accent was an intriguing mix of Texan and brougeish, and sometimes, like when she'd said the Scottish staple affirmative, no one could've convinced Graeme she wasn't a native.

He liked her very much.

"So, does that mean your sister is kind of related to me?"

Claire laughed and nodded. "I guess so!"

"Where're my kinfolk?" A booming voice in a Highland brogue announced, as another very large, dark-haired man entered the great hall, with two women on his heels. He also wore a plaid.

Graeme recognized it as MacDonald Clan tartan, and he smiled. His grandfather had a blanket and various other items covered in the same pattern in his house.

"Jules!" Claire called, waving her sister over. "That's them. Laird and Lady MacDonald." She giggled, as if she couldn't keep her amusement at bay.

Lexi dashed across the hall and practically tackled the girl with the couple. She had to be Brenna, Claire's niece.

Even from the distance, he could tell she was gorgeous, and her hair was about the same sandy color as his. Which amused him, since he'd always associated his lighter hair with his mother's side. Although, how much like him and Gramps could seventeenth century ancestors be, really?

"There're too many MacDonalds in my hall," Duncan quipped, a playful smirk on his lips.

"'Tis *my* hall," Alex retorted.

Claire caught Graeme's eye and rolled hers.

He grinned again.

Hugh MacDonald matched the MacLeod males in height and breadth, and had a firm shake. He offered a smile when they met officially, one Gramps and Graeme returned. He almost gasped at the man's very dark brown eyes, the exact same as theirs.

Jules was open and friendly, hugging them both, while Brenna was shy, a pretty pink blush on her cheeks when her father introduced her.

She had her father's dark eyes, and she was strikingly beautiful. She was a few years younger than Lexi, if Graeme remembered correctly, but her father probably had to actively keep all the male interest away.

"I'm so glad ye could come fer my weddin'," Lexi said, holding both of Jules' hands.

"Oh, we wouldn't miss it, sweetie." Jules wasn't Lexi's blood aunt, but she always referred to her as such.

Graeme would've never guessed a family from the past was so close and normal with each other. Smiles, laughs, physical affection. It was all there, even between Alex, Duncan and Hugh. They might tease and chide, but they cared for each other deeply, easily seen through their interactions. Something Graeme had had all his life, and had missed very much since he'd lost his parents.

They all obviously enjoyed each other's company, and besides Angus and little Iain, Lexi and her three male cousins were close in age and had grown up together.

He hadn't been able to tear his gaze away from her,

despite the intriguing environment. Lexi wore a baby-pink gown with a tight bodice, her cleavage on prominent display.

Alex had frowned when she'd arrived in the great hall in the dress. She'd changed from the simple shift she'd put on at the beach. His love had ignored her father's ire. It was the night before her wedding, she'd said, and she'd wear what she wanted.

Hugh growled, and all eyes landed on him.

Graeme blinked. The man's demeanor changed so drastically, so quickly.

What the hell had happened?

"He dinnae need be wed in tha'!" The MacDonald laird scowled, pointing at Graeme, as if he was covered in shit. "I forbid it. He's a *MacDonald*."

"Calm your jets, my laird," Claire said, but seemed to struggle not to laugh.

Graeme arched an eyebrow. "What's his deal?" he tried to whisper, but it was more of the stage variety.

"You're wearing the wrong plaid, at least in my husband's opinion," Jules replied, holding back a laugh. Her full mouth rippled; her green eyes danced. The older woman's hair was honey-colored, darker than her sister's, and she wore it in a simple knot, gathered at the back of her head. She was pretty, like her daughter, and Claire.

"The wedding isn't until tomorrow, Hugh. He can dress MacDonald colors then," Claire said.

"I'll see ta it," the big man barked.

Graeme presented both his palms, high. "I don't want to impose—"

"I'll see ta it," his ancestor repeated, even harder and louder.

There was no sense in fighting a MacDonald, if his previous arguments with Gramps were any indication.

"Sorry, my daughter's betrothed's attire dinnae suit," Alex said, but there was a twinkle in his eyes that shouted his insincerity.

"Aye, we dinnae have MacDonald plaid jus' lyin' 'round," Duncan cosigned, gesturing around the hall.

The MacDonald laird glared, his dark eyes and his expression even darker.

Graeme bit his lip to keep from laughing, as not to piss off another oversized dude that owned more than one claymore. Especially a distant blood relative.

Lexi slid her hand in his, and even her eyes danced with laughter.

"Weel, everaone's here. Let us feast!" Alex announced.

The evening melted into night, and after dinner and some music, MacLeods started drifting off to their beds. Gramps and Graeme were shown to guest rooms not far from each other, and Graeme made sure his grandfather was settled before stripping out of the material that had offended his MacDonald ancestor so greatly.

There was already a folded MacDonald plaid resting at the end of the bed on top of a trunk, in the sizable room. Hugh had sent for it from his home, Armadale Castle, immediately, and it had arrived not long ago.

He pitied the guy that'd had to make that ride at top speed just to come right back to Dunvegan over a piece of clothing. It was wasted hours, but he knew better than to argue with the big man. Besides, it would make Graeme proud to wear his family's plaid on the day he married the love of his life.

At least in 1694. When they returned to the twenty-first century, they'd have to make the marriage legal, and somehow get Lexi an ID. Maybe her magic could come in handy for that.

The MacDonald laird also given Graeme a white leine which was a much finer material than the one he'd borrowed from Angus. It must be what passed for a dress-shirt, circa seventeenth century.

Hugh and Jules had also extended an invitation to Graeme and Gramps to visit Armadale, and his grandfather had barely waited for the laird to finish speaking before yelling, *"Aye!"*

Seeing his own ancestral home would be an honor for sure, and Graeme looked forward to it, too.

For his wedding, Angus had promised to help him dress in the morning. He'd need a few lessons before he could put on a plaid by himself.

He'd just crawled into the big, borrowed bed when an appealing petite form slipped into the room and closed the door quietly.

"If your father catches you in here, I might not have my bollocks for our wedding," Graeme said, but he wasn't upset that his love had snuck into his guest room.

Lexi giggled. "I barred the door." Her oversized

ivory shirt fell to her knees.

Despite the dimness in the room, the light from the fireplace revealed a hint of her gorgeous silhouette, teasing him.

Damn, he wanted her.

"And? I bet he could ram his shoulder into it, and it would pop right open. Then he'd cut off my head with that huge sword. Or worse, my dick."

She put her hand over her mouth to cover more laughter.

He couldn't help his smile, and certainly didn't turn her way when she crawled into the borrowed bed and snuggled into his side.

"My da is fond a' ye now. 'Twill be okay, as ye say."

Graeme arched an eyebrow. "I doubt it."

"I dinnae plan ta get caught." Lexi's playful eyes held a dare.

He caressed her jaw and urged her mouth up to his. He'd meant the kiss to be light, but it melded into something serious and hot. He was hard and aching in only a few thumps of his heart.

"But you, my darlin', are *not* quiet when I'm inside you."

Lexi shuddered in his arms, shooting a bolt of desire into his already throbbing balls. The shirt shifted, and one of her shoulders was bare. Her breasts were so perfect and soft, already pressing into his chest.

He was lost her, like he couldn't wait to be for the rest of his life. "You don't think it's bad luck to see me before the wedding?"

She arched an eyebrow. "Nay, why?"

"It's just a saying from my time. Never mind." He shook his head and smirked. When had such a silly concept started anyway? Graeme would have to look it up when they got home.

He got her naked in seconds and kissed her into oblivion.

Lexi was so sweet and responsive to his touch, like always.

Yet, somehow this time together, everything felt like *more*.

They made love slowly, with no urgency. Only kisses and touches and perfection at first, until they cascaded over the edge together.

"*Tha gaol agam ort*," she breathed in Gaelic against his mouth, panting as they came back down.

"I love you, too." Graeme caressed her cheeks, then pulled her even closer. Running his hand up and down her back felt like the most natural thing in the world, like the rhythm of his heartbeat against hers.

He didn't know much of his ancestors' language, but translating what she'd said was easy, and he'd heard the phrase that evening, because it was something Alex had whispered to Alana. Lexi had promised to teach him if he wanted. He did, and Gramps would approve, too.

Her fingertips tickled through his chest hair as she nestled her head on his pec.

"Are you sure about this?" he asked, breaking a companionable silence.

"Marryin' ye?" Lexi asked, lifting her head from his chest.

He chuckled. "No. Staying here for the night."

"Oh, aye."

"Uh, should I be offended that you just asked me if I thought you still wanted to marry me?" Graeme teased.

She shrugged, but couldn't hide her grin. A new dare glinted in her violet eyes again. "Maybe I dinnae be sure, until ye kiss me again."

He growled and flipped them, tucking her beneath him, and doing just that.

the end

about the author

USA Today Bestselling, award winning author of romantic suspense, epic and historical fantasy romance, C.A. loves to dabble in different genres. If it's a good story, she'll write it, no matter where it seems to fit!

She's a hopeless romantic and always will be. Risking it all for Happily Ever After is what she lives by!

C.A. is originally from Ohio, but got to Texas as soon as she could. She's happily married and has a bachelor's degree in Criminal Justice.

She's always writing, and helps small business owners by writing their websites, and she loves it!

WEBSITE: http://www.caszarek.com
EBOOK STORE: https://www.caszarek.com/ebook-store
PAPERBACK STORE:
https://www.caszarek.com/paperback-store
FACEBOOK: http://www.facebook.com/caszarek
INSTAGRAM: https://www.instagram.com/caszarek/
TWITTER: https://twitter.com/caszarek
BOOKBUB: https://www.bookbub.com/profile/c-a-szarek
GOODREADS:https://www.goodreads.com/author/show/5815085.C_A_Szarek
EMAIL: ca@caszarek.com

You can sign up for C.A.'s newsletter on her website, as well as buy all her books!

CPSIA information can be obtained
at www.ICGtesting.com
Printed in the USA
BVHW041248200822
645045BV00001B/53

9 781941 151426